A LEGEND IS BORN

Suddenly there was the sound of running bootsteps behind Shattuck. He stopped, but before he could turn, gunfire thundered and bracketed him. Bullet-riddled, he staggered forward, then fell.

Howie Dryden laughed wildly. "I got him! I got the murderous bastid!" he yelled.

This was the beginning of the reputation that would probably lead Howie Dryden to a coward's grave on Boot Hill. . . .

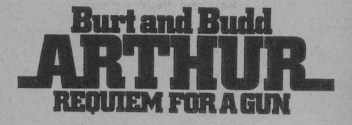

Burt and Budd

ARTHUR

REQUIEM FOR A GUN

AVON
PUBLISHERS OF BARD, CAMELOT, DISCUS, EQUINOX AND FLARE BOOKS

AVON BOOKS
A division of
The Hearst Corporation
959 Eighth Avenue
New York, New York 10019

ISBN: 0-380-00240-X

First Avon Printing, August, 1963
Fifth Printing

AVON TRADEMARK REG. U.S. PAT. OFF. AND
FOREIGN COUNTRIES, REGISTERED TRADEMARK—
MARCA REGISTRADA, HECHO EN CHICAGO, U.S.A.

Printed in the U.S.A.

ONE

It was shortly before eight o'clock in the morning. It was a little too early for any of Deedee Farnum's regular customers to hurry in for their customary eye openers. It was much too early for the old men and the town's idlers who hung around the saloon for want of something better to do to start drifting in. There was only one customer in the place, and he was a stranger. He stood at the shiny new bar, about halfway down its length, hunched over it with his shoulders rounded, his elbows resting on the curved lip, and the run-down heel of his right boot hooked over the foot rail. Other boots had already scuffed it and this added to its defacement. There was a half-drained glass of beer in front of him. He toyed with it, rolled the glass gently between his big hands, swishing the beer about till it frothed and foam-ringed the inside of the glass. His hat, his shirt, pants and boots, his wind-burned, sun-bronzed face too, all were flaked with fine alkali dust, evidence that he had ridden long and far. There was grey in his sideburns and the lines in his face were long and deeply etched, almost like knife slashes. He wore his gun low slung and thong-tied around his lean right thigh, the holster open-ended at the bottom and cut away at the top. His gunbelt was made of thick, heavy leather and so was the holster that hung from it. Both were hand-tooled and studded with penny-sized pieces of silver and colored stones, the recognizable work of skilled Mexican silversmiths and leather workers. Tinier bits of silver were imbedded in the jutting butt of his gun.

The bartender, bald-headed Pat Fry, who was addicted to celluloid collars, string bow-ties and fancy rosetted sleeve garters, was stacking upended glasses on a towel-covered shelf below the mirror on the wall behind the bar. He glanced at his lone customer a couple of times. But the latter was too deeply occupied with his thoughts to notice. Once and then a second time, Fry, who was a friendly and talk-ative individual, took a step toward him, intending to say something to draw him into conversation. But each time something stayed him, made him hesitate and reconsider. As a result, he held his tongue and went on with what he was doing. There was something about the man, some-thing that Fry couldn't quite put his finger on, that warned him not to intrude upon the stranger and his absorbing thoughts.

It was only when three men and a fourth one who fol-lowed them at something of a foot-dragging distance entered the saloon that the man at the bar straightened up. He was taller than Fry had thought him, and he was rangy too. When he met the bartender's glance, Fry saw a forbidding glint in his cold, steely eyes, and he was glad he hadn't forced himself upon him. The newcomers were cattlemen. They were the Strang brothers, Milt, Merve and Mike. The fourth man was Howie Dryden, their hired hand. Milt, who was the oldest, was big and beefy, while his brothers were only about average height and build. Dryden, who was painfully thin and awkwardly lanky, looked nervous and apprehensive. Milt halted a couple of steps inside the saloon with the others behind him filling the open doorway. When he gestured, Mike, the youngest of the Strangs, turned and practically herded the plainly reluctant Dryden ahead of him, guided Dryden around the back-turned stranger and stopped with him a dozen or so feet farther down the bar. Together they squared around. As Fry looked on won-deringly, Merve stepped around Milt and started to back against the far side wall. When Milt gestured, Merve and he exchanged places so that while Merve blocked the doorway, Milt was directly opposite the man who had become the object of their maneuvering. Milt shot a quick look at his companions. Obviously satisfied that they were in position, he said curtly:

"Turn around, mister."

Suddenly sensing what the Strangs were up to, Fry said protestingly as he started to come out from behind the bar:

"Now hold it a minute, you fellers. I don't know what this is all about, and I don't wanna know. But Deedee's laid out a lot o' dough fixing up this place and you haven't any

6

right to go bustin' it up on him. So whatever you're aiming to do, don't do it in here. G'wan outside where there's plenty o' room and . . ."

"Better get yourself outta here, Pat," Milt said stonily, interrupting him. "And you'd better do it now."

Fry was motionless for a moment. Then he began to retreat behind the bar. He stopped when he came to the far end of it, within the thin shadows of the back room.

"Turn around, mister," Milt ordered a second time.

The stranger turned slowly, and backing against the bar, rested his elbows on it. His hands hung loosely from his wrists with the right hand, the fingers spread apart and curled the barest bit, dangling a little lower than the left. His glance took in the four men who were facing him.

"Your name's Shattuck, isn't it?" Milt asked him.

The man nodded and said:

"That's right." Then with a little smile in which his thin lips alone participated, he said, "The way you men are standing around me, somebody looking in here might get the idea that you're fixin' to brace me."

"We're going to kill you, Shattuck," Milt told him grimly.

"Just like that, huh?"

"Remember a young feller named Matty Strang?"

Shattuck thought a moment, shook his head and answered:

"Nope. Never heard of him."

. "He was only a kid, a nice looking kid too. He'd just topped nineteen. He didn't stand a chance against you and you must've known it. You could have winged him and let him off that way. But you didn't. You shot him dead."

Shattuck held his tongue.

"That was nearly four years ago," Milt said. "When we got word of what you'd done, we started out after you. But by then it was too late. You had too much of a jump on us. So you got away. But we knew you'd show back here one day and that all we had to do was wait. No gun slinger ever stays put anywhere for long. He keeps moving on all the time because no place is home to him. And pretty soon he forgets the places he's been and starts making the rounds all over again. So y'see, being patient and willing to wait has paid off for us."

"Tell me something, mister," Shattuck said, interrupting

7

him. "Would this kid, this Matty Strang or whatever his name was, would he have been satisfied with winging me, or only with killing me?"

"That hasn't anything to do with it!"

"It hasn't, huh?" Shattuck retorted. "The way you see it, I'm supposed to let every hairbrained kid potshot me and I'm supposed to like it. Wanna know something, mister? In just about every town I hit, soon's word that I'm there gets around, some snot-nosed kid who thinks he's fast with a gun and has a hankering for a big reputation gets the itch to try me on for size. Every one o' th'm figures the same way, that he's faster'n I am and that it's his big chance to prove it and make a name for himself. All he's gotta do is gun me down. I don't remember any Matty Strang. What I do remember about this town is that some kid kept dogging me every which way I turned and kept daring me to stand and fight. I remember warning him, telling him what would happen to him if he didn't quit. But it didn't do any good. He kept following me and when he began to crowd me too hard, there wasn't anything I could do but take him on. He begged for it and he got it."

"I still say you didn't have to kill him!" Milt insisted.

"Y'know, instead o' putting all the blame on me for what happened, why don't you face up to it and admit you were just as much to blame? Maybe it was even more your fault than mine, y'know? How come you didn't try to get him to understand that when anybody, man or boy, goes looking for trouble, he usu'lly winds up with a helluva lot more than he bargained for? I think you've been nursing a guilty conscience all these years, mister, and that now you think you're gonna square things all around, although more for yourself than that kid, by killing me."

Apparently Milt Strang had no ready reply for him. So he just glowered at Shattuck.

"I've let others off the hook when I should've killed them and saved myself a lotta grief, and you wanna know what happened with each one?" Shattuck went on. "I'd have a run-in with some fresh young squirt and wing him in the arm. Soon's he got over it and was able to hold his gun again, I'm damned if he didn't start trackin' me and when he caught up with me, it always wound up the same way. In a shoot-out. Got so, every town I'd come to, there was

8

somebody waiting and layin' for me. This kid Matty, what was he to you, your son?"

"My brother!" was the indignant reply.

"Your son or your brother, what difference does it make? None that I can see. We-ll, we've both had our say. Now what d'we do?"

Milt didn't answer.

"Mean you still wanna go through with this, huh? All right. I was kinda hoping you'd have better sense. But if you're in such a sweat to die, it's all right with me. Just think this over before you go for your gun. I'll get a couple of you, maybe even more than just two of you, while you're getting me. And you know who I'm gonna get first, don't you? You, mister. I'm gonna give it to you right smack in that pot belly of yours. You'll get a chance to see what your guts look like when they spill out on the floor." Shattuck shot a look at Merve. "Who's he?"

"My brother," Milt said stiffly.

"That's too bad. And him?" Shattuck asked, indicating Mike Strang with a jerk of his head. "He your brother too?"

"Yes."

"They in such a sweat to die too, or did you talk them into thinking they are?" There was no reply. "What about that character?" Shattuck wanted to know about Dryden.

"He rides for us."

"He doesn't look like much to me. Fact is, he looks scared to death. Don't count on him for much, Strang. I wouldn't if I were you."

There was no response from Milt. With another quick glance at his companions, he backed a little more till his shoulders were nudging the wall.

"All right," Shattuck said. "I'm ready whenever you are."

"Now!" Milt yelled.

Instantly Pat Fry dropped on all fours behind the bar. There was a deafening roar of gunfire. The building seemed to rock on its shallow foundation. The stacked glasses tinkled and shattered when a wildly fired bullet chipped out a piece of the wall mirror and the gouged out piece struck the glasses. A second bullet, fired from a different direction, struck the mirror squarely and cracked it from one end to the other. Oddly, though, the crack ran ruler-

9

straight for only a few inches on either side of the actual point of contact. After that it seemed to waver, and ran crookedly, like one of Deedee's customers weaving a late hour rubbery-legged course homeward. The shooting ended abruptly although the echoes of the blended shots hung in the air for a couple of moments and then gently lifted even higher and faded out. The building settled back on its haunches with something that sounded like a sigh of relief.

Fry raised up slowly and cautiously peered out over the bar. Milt Strang, impaled momentarily on the wall by the impact of a bullet slamming into him and drilling through his beefy body, slid down to the floor and lay still. His gun was still gripped in his thick, fleshy hand. His hat had come off, probably jarred off when he collided with the wall, and lay just beyond him. Blood had begun to ebb out of him. Fry, staring with wide eyes, saw a thin rivulet seep out from under him and run along a thin crack between two floorboards. There was no sign of Merve Strang and Fry wondered what had become of him. He turned his gaze in the other direction. Howie Dryden, his face a pasty, bloodless white, had thrown down his gun and stood with his empty hands raised. Mike Strang was on his knees, head bowed against the bar, with his shattered right arm hanging limply at his side. He had dropped his gun. It lay barely six inches from Dryden's.

Just as Fry emerged from behind the bar there was body movement in front of it, and he stopped instantly and stared hard. Rising from a crouch was Shattuck. His leveled gun, the muzzle of it fire-blackened, was clutched in his hand. There was a bloody streak across his cheek where a bullet had creased and furrowed it. He glanced at Milt, turned his head and looked at Mike, gave Dryden a scornful look, turned his back on him and holstered his gun.

"You'd better get him to a doctor," he said to Fry, jerking his right thumb over his shoulder in Mike's direction. "You heard them, didn't you?"

"Yeah, sure."

"Then you know I didn't start it. I'm counting on you to tell that to the sheriff."

Fry nodded and said again:

10

"Yeah, sure. I'll tell him."

"Suppose you go get him and bring him back here. Then you can take him," and again he indicated Mike, this time though with a half-turn of his body and a nod, "to the doctor."

"Right," Fry said, turned and trudged out with his long apron flapping around his ankles. But a moment later he reappeared in the open doorway. "Y'got Merve too, mister. He's layin' in the gutter up the street a ways."

Suddenly there was a converging rush of booted feet and wide-eyed men massed behind Fry and stared in.

"Never mind, Mac," Shattuck said to Fry. "I'll go get the sheriff and bring him back with me and you can tell him what happened."

The bartender moved aside to permit Shattuck to pass. A path opened for him through the onlookers. Heads turned and eyes followed him as he started up the street. He stopped when he came up to where Merve Strang lay in the gutter, slumped over on his side. He stood for a long moment looking down at him, then he went on again. Suddenly there were running bootsteps behind him. He stopped. But before he could turn or look back, gunfire thundered and bracketed him, and bullet-riddled, he staggered brokenly out to the curb and perched on it, swayed over it. Once or twice it appeared that he was about to pitch out into the gutter; but somehow each time he managed to steady himself, and finally moved back onto the narrow walk. His legs buckled under him and he tottered, then slowly sank to his knees and gently slid forward across the planking on his face with his empty hands hanging over the curb. The man who had burst out of the saloon after him, a tall, lanky man who ran with an awkward stride, came skidding up to him. Gun in hand, he bent over Shattuck, peered closely into the fallen gun fighter's face, and nudged him with his gun. When Shattuck did not move, the man came erect again, holstered his gun and stepped back. Suddenly, though, he bent again and spat at the sprawled figure at his feet. Straightening up, he cast a triumphal look at the men who were massed on the walk in front of the saloon watching him.

He laughed a little wildly and yelled:

"I got him all right! I got the bastid!"

With a heave of his narrow and uneven shoulders, he strode back to the saloon, laughing a little to himself all the while and patting the holstered gun that rode on his hip.

TWO

The following morning when Fry was sweeping off the walk in front of the saloon, the rhythmic thump of boots on the planking made him stay his broom, turn his head and look in the direction of the man who was approaching him. Fry recognized him at once. It was the sheriff, Win Tuttle. Crossing his folded arms on the broom handle, Fry waited till the wiry, grey-haired lawman came up to him, nodded and said:

"Morning, Sheriff."

Tuttle grunted.

"Kinda early for you to be up and doing, isn't it?" he asked rather grumpily. His tone reflected his need for his coffee with which to brighten his disposition. He had been known to admit he was not the pleasantest individual before he had had his breakfast and couldn't understand people who were. In fact, he was inclined to look upon them with suspicion. "Must be for a change you got up before breakfast."

The bartender grinned at him.

"You must've too," he replied.

"H'm," Tuttle said.

Lifting his gaze past Fry, he ranged it over the somewhat crookedly laid out street that spread away before him. There was no one about as yet, no sound of anyone either. He found himself staring critically at the buildings that framed the hushed street. They were old, flimsily constructed, drab and weatherbeaten. He couldn't remember the last time he had seen anyone doing any repairing or painting. Yet there wasn't a single building within range of his eyes that wasn't in need of something. In the raw late dawn and pre-morning light that revealed its deficiencies in painful detail, the town looked so shabby it made him frown darkly. He wondered why he hadn't noticed it before.

13

He had heard of towns dying of neglect. But because he had no intention of letting this one die, he would see to it, he told himself grimly, that the shopkeepers and townspeople did something about it. He was just about to say something to that effect to Pat Fry when he saw a woman weighed down by a heavy water bucket appear at the head of an alley. She stopped abruptly and looked down at herself when some of the water sloshed over her.

Turning her head, she shrilled to someone whom the lawman could not see:

"You lazy, drunken bum! You good for nothing! On account o' you I just got myself a good wetting!"

"G'wan, y'old crow!" a man yelled back at her in a throaty, raspy voice.

Tuttle grunted again and said:

"The Winikers are at it again."

"What d'you mean 'again'? They're always at it, always fussin' and hollering. Doesn't make a damned bit o' difference to them whether it's morning or night. They yap and yowl at each other like a couple o' mountain cats."

The sheriff had nothing to say. Straightening up, Fry turned his head and looked down the street too. Using both of her hands, Tillie Winiker carried the bucket out to the curb and put it down at the very edge of it, stepped behind the bucket and with a sudden thrust of her foot, overturned it. The water gushed into the gutter, muddying it, filling and overflowing the deep ruts. Bending over the bucket, she tilted it, emptying it, and straightening up again, plodded back with it to the alley and disappeared. The two men turned to each other.

"When's Deedee supposed to get back?" Tuttle asked.

"He should be in on this afternoon's stage. But I don't mind telling you I'm not looking forward to seeing him. When he gets a look at that new mirror, he'll have a fit."

"He'll get over it," the sheriff said curtly. "Wasn't your fault that it got broke. It was the Strangs' doing. So he can get after Mike Strang to make good for it."

"Yeah," Fry conceded. "Only trouble is, Deedee's the kind who has to holler first. Then after a while when he runs outta breath, he kinda simmers down a mite while he's getting his second wind. That's when I'll try to tell him what happened." When there was no response from

14

Tuttle, Fry said, "Hear you had something of a to-do last night with Howie Dryden."

"Chased him outta town."

"So I heard."

"I never did cotton to that hungry-lookin' polecat. And the longer I thought about the way he cut down Shattuck from behind, the less I liked it and him. Finally got myself worked up enough to tell him to get his gear and clear out."

"Sorry I missed it."

"You didn't miss much," Tuttle assured him. "Dryden ran off some at the mouth. When I'd heard enough outta that side-winder, I pulled him up short and told him to start riding. He knew I meant business, so he got going. But just to show you how some people's minds work and what kind o' locoed ideas some o' th'm can come up with, listen to this. Dryden felt that instead o' me chasing him outta town, I shoulda got everybody together and got them to give him some token of our appreciation. You know, for ridding us of Len Shattuck."

Fry grinned broadly and asked:

"What d'you suppose he had in mind, a medal? Or d'you suppose he was thinking of something bigger, say like a statue?"

"He didn't say and I didn't ask him," the sheriff retorted. But then his tone changed again as he resumed his recital. "I don't deny that I'm glad Shattuck's dead. But I'll say this for him. I never heard of him making the first move against anybody. It was always the other feller who drew first. So while the law didn't exactly approve of Len Shattuck, it never had any reason to go after him. Man's got the right to defend himself and that's what Shattuck did."

"Only he was too fast with his gun for those who set out to take him."

"That's right," Tuttle agreed. "But times have changed. Fact is, they keep changing every day, and for the better. More and more men have quit wearing guns because they've come to the point where they're willing to talk things out instead o' shooting 'em out."

"I've been noticing that too."

As though he hadn't heard Fry's comment, Tuttle added: "So the day of the gun slinger is about over. That's why

15

I said it's just as well that Shattuck's gone. He was outta step with the changing times, and he was too old and too set in his ways to change."

"How about his gun? Did you find it?"

The lawman frowned.

"Nope. I've asked all around, but nobody seems to know what became of it."

"Funny, isn't it?"

"Not to me it isn't," Tuttle shot back at Fry. "I don't like the idea of having Shattuck's gun loose. No good can come of it. When a gun slinger cashes in, I think his gun oughta be buried with him because the two belong together. This way . . ."

"But what could've happened to it?"

"What d'you think happened to it?" Tuttle demanded. "A gun doesn't just up and fly away. Somebody with takin' ways took it."

"Yeah, but what for? What would anybody want with it, 'specially with Shattuck's initials on it?"

"Way I see it, there are, we-ll, three kinds of men who would want that gun. One's the kind who'd want it for, well, to haul out and show off for company years from now and probably with a cock 'n bull story to go with it about how he came to get hold of it. Maybe even how he took it away from Shattuck. Depending on how much of a liar he is. That kind's all talk and doesn't worry me though."

"But the other two do, huh?"

The sheriff nodded.

"Next is the kind that always aimed to be big and important but never made the grade," he continued. "Take a man like that, a man who's bitter because his life's been a bust and a disappointment to him, put a gun like Shattuck's in his hand, give his imagination a chance to build, and there's no telling how far he's liable to let himself get carried away by it."

"Mean he's liable to think that just by wearing Shattuck's gun it'll make him another Shattuck?"

"Could be."

"All he'll have to do then is go looking for trouble and somebody'll cut him down to the size he was before."

Tuttle shrugged and went on:

"The third kind's the worst. Some young squirt who

16

thinks he's fast with his gun. Up to now he's stayed in line. Let him get hold of Shattuck's gun and there'll be no holding him back. He'll go looking for somebody to use it on and he won't care who that somebody might be. And that includes me."

"We've got a couple like that around here. Young uns who are too big for their britches even though they're still wet behind the ears. Like Will Hewitt's kid, Robbie, and that widow's boy, that Mrs. Anderson's Phil. They're the troublesome kind all right. Too bad they don't go after each other. That'd save you some trouble, wouldn't it?"

"Yeah, guess it would," the sheriff admitted. But quickly he added, "But don't go looking for that to happen. I know I won't. That'd make my job too easy. After all these years of having to go it alone and taking on all kinds of ornery critters, homegrown and others from other places, I wouldn't know what to make of it. So because I don't look for miracles to happen, if that Robbie Hewitt and that Anderson boy start acting up, do I have to tell you whose job it'll be to? . . ."

"Albie Smith," Fry said, interrupting him. "Coming over here."

Tuttle turned his head and leveled his gaze at a big, burly, barrel-chested man who wore a leather apron hanging from around his neck and tied on around his ample middle and who was coming diagonally across the street from the direction of the stable and blacksmith's shop. Presently the man was standing before Tuttle.

"Got something to tell you, Sheriff," he began without any preliminaries.

"Go ahead and tell me."

"You don't have to do any more lookin' around for that Shattuck feller's gun. I know who's got it."

"Oh, you do, huh?" Tuttle shot back at him, bristlingly. "How come you didn't tell me last night when I asked you?"

"Because I only found out just now," Smith answered calmly. Some of the burning went out of the sheriff's angry eyes. "Fact is, no more'n a couple o' minutes ago."

"Oh," Tuttle said grumpily. "Who's got it?"

"Seems old Timmy Jordan . . ."

"Don't tell me it was that mangy old drunk who swiped

17

it? Where is he? Over at your place? I'll go haul him out and skin him alive!"

Smith frowned.

"You wanna hear what I've got to say, or don't you?" he demanded. The sheriff flushed a little, but wisely held his tongue. Then the brawny stableman went on in a more moderate tone. "Timmy had the gun. But he hasn't got it now."

"Doggone it, Albie!" Tuttle, unable to restrain himself any longer, sputtered impatiently. "If he hasn't got it, then who in blazes has got it?"

"That Howie Dryden."

The sheriff stared at him. After a moment, though, he gulped, and grimacing, swallowed hard.

"Dryden, huh?" he echoed in a strained, wheezing voice.

"That's right. Y'see, Sheriff, I don't pay Timmy anything for the little odd jobs he does for me around the stable. Can't afford to. Don't do that much business. So I give him his three squares and a place to bed down for the night. The hay loft. How he came to get hold of the gun, I don't know. He didn't say and I didn't ask. All I know is that when Dryden, who musta known somehow that Timmy had it, offered him ten bucks for the gun, Timmy made the swap right then and there. Been so long since he had 'ny dough of his own, Dryden's ten bucks musta looked like a thousand to him. Anyway, that's the story of what happened to Shattuck's gun."

"Swell story, all right," Tuttle retorted. "I chased Dryden outta town last night and by now he's probably put thirty, forty miles between him and us. And the first town he hits, I'll bet you anything you like that Shattuck's gun will be riding in his holster. On top o' that, he'll be making like he's Shattuck."

"So what?" Fry who had been standing quietly at the lawman's side asked him. "If he talks outta turn to somebody who calls him on it, wearing Shattuck's gun and makin' like he's Shattuck won't help him one little bit. He'll get his teeth kicked out. But that'll be his tough luck. Not yours. So the hell with him and the same for the gun. And instead o' you lookin' so put out, you oughta be damned glad to be rid of both o' them."

Before Tuttle could answer, the grinding rumble of

wagon wheels and the pounding beat of horses' hoofs that lifted and carried in the chilly air made the three men turn and look up the street. They saw a stagecoach hauled by four galloping horses wheel into town, saw the driver, perched on the wide seat of the swaying, top-heavy vehicle, pull back on the lines and slow the prancing horses to a trot. As they watched, the stage came to a screeching stop in front of the stage company depot, a couple of doors upstreet from the sheriff's office.

"What are they doing, running a morning stage now instead of the afternoon?" Fry asked.

"All I know is what I see," Tuttle replied. "If they wanna change their schedule, that's their business and I don't aim to make it mine."

They saw the driver wind the reins around the handbrake and climb down, saw him yank open the coach door and help a bonneted woman to the ground. When a big, overdressed, paunchy man carrying a small satchel climbed out and stood in the gutter for a moment, apparently criticizing or complaining about something to the driver, Fry recognized him at once and groaned.

"Deedee," he said with an unhappy shake of his head. "And here ahead of time. I've been sorta building myself up to having him light into me this afternoon. After I've had something to eat. I can take it better when my belly's full. But I haven't even had my breakfast yet, and here he is, mad-lookin' as usual. And if that driver sassed him any, I'll catch it good. Takes everything out on me. We-ll," he said with a sigh of resignation, "long as he's gonna holler, he might as well start in on me inside after he's had a look at that busted mirror. Then he'll really have something to holler about."

There was no response, no word of encouragement from the sheriff or from Albie Smith. Hoisting his broom to his shoulder, Fry trudged into the saloon.

THREE

Some thirty-one miles farther westward, in the very heart of the grassy flatlands, the quiet, peaceful little cattle town of Macum lay half in shadows and half in thin but rapidly brightening sunshine. It was only about eight-thirty, much too early for the sun to dissolve the shadows. By noon-time though it would be directly overhead, the shadows would be burned away, the town would be bathed in dazzling sunshine, and all outdoor activity would cease. But by about four o'clock the sun would have moved on and all activity would be resumed. In Andy Horvath's saloon, located in the very middle of the short and almost stubby single street that was the town, a lone customer, Howie Dryden, was hunched over the bar with his long-fingered, bony hands wrapped around a foam-ringed beer glass that he had just drained. When an aproned store-keeper suddenly appeared in the open doorway, called to Horvath and beckoned excitedly, the saloonkeeper emerged from behind the bar and strode to the door and listened attentively to what the gesticulating and breathless store-keeper had to tell him. When the storekeeper finished, stepped back and scurried away, Horvath, a well-built man of about fifty, frowning darkly, slowly returned to his place behind the bar. Backed against the mirrored wall he fixed his gaze on the doorway. A couple of times he shifted his gaze and peered streetward through the window, once craning his neck for a better view. When he squared around and found Dryden eyeing him wonderingly, he said:

"Sheriff died a couple of days ago and we haven't got around yet to pickin' somebody else for the job. But somehow some young gun thrower musta found out about it and rode in a while ago and from what I've been told aims to take over. He oughta be coming in here any min-

20

ute now. That's why I keep looking outside. To see if he's coming."

"Uh-huh," Dryden said mechanically, rather than with any show of interest.

"Understand he's been making the rounds, telling the storekeepers how much it's gonna cost each one to stay open and do business here."

Dryden's shaggy eyebrows arched a bit.

"That's nice."

"He's got a helluva lot o' gall, if you ask me," Horvath retorted.

This time there was no response from Dryden. Deciding that it might be wise for him to move on before there was any trouble, he straightened up, slapped a coin on the bar and turned to go. He stopped abruptly when a slim youth wearing his gun low and tied down appeared in the doorway, ranged a quick look around the place, stepped inside and came sauntering up to the bar with a nod to Dryden and a friendly, boyish smile to Horvath. He wore a new Stetson, a light tannish thing, tilted rather rakishly over his right eye, blue levis and a lighter blue shirt. Both the levis and the shirt looked tailor-made. Only his boots looked worn, almost run-down. There was something that Dryden couldn't quite make out woven in dark blue thread above the youth's shirt pocket. It was only when he halted within touching distance of Dryden that the weaving above his pocket focussed into a name: Clete Ainslee. He rested his hands on the lip of the bar.

"Nice little town you've got here," he said to Horvath.

"We like it," the saloonkeeper replied.

"Just the kind I've been looking for," Ainslee went on. "Nice and quiet. This the only saloon in town?"

"That's right."

"Then you must do all right here."

Horvath held his tongue. Ainslee eyed the gun in Howie Dryden's holster, peered at the pin-scratched initials in the heel plate, and said:

"That's quite a gun you've got there, mister. Mind if I have a look at it?" Before the slow-reacting Dryden could answer or put out a restraining hand, the youth lifted the gun out of the holster, examined it, nodded and said, "Yes, it's quite a gun."

"Something you want, young feller?" Horvath asked him.

Ainslee gave him another smile that revealed small, white, perfectly formed teeth, and nodded.

"It's going to cost you fifty dollars a month to do business here," he said evenly, pointing the gun at Horvath. "And being that this is collection day, I'll take it now."

"Not from me you won't," Horvath said grimly.

The gun exploded with such startling and deafening suddenness that Dryden, wincing, jerked backward from the bar. Glass shattered behind Horvath's head and fell, tinklingly.

"Next time I'll put a bullet right between your eyes," Ainslee told him. He gestured with the gun and held out his left hand and snapped his fingers impatiently. "Come on, get it up and hand it over."

Andy Horvath, pale-faced and tight-lipped, did not move. The slim youth, still holding the gun on him, whirled around the bar, crunching bits of glass under his boots, drove Horvath back at gun-point, jerked open the cash drawer and looked in it.

"Only some change in here," he said. He turned to Horvath. "Where's the money?"

"Where you can't get it. In the bank."

Ainslee looked hard at him for a tensed moment as Dryden shuttled his gaze between the two. Suddenly Ainslee lashed out at Horvath with the gun, struck him viciously in the face with it, followed Horvath as the latter staggered backward and gun-whipped him about the face and head. It was only when the saloonkeeper, reeling drunkenly under the savage beating, his face a battered, crimsoned mass, finally fell that Ainslee stopped. Backing out from behind the bar, he turned and headed for the door, stopped within a stride of it, looked back at Dryden, who was staring at him with wide eyes and gaping mouth, and said:

"The last time I saw this gun, Len Shattuck, the man who owned it and whose initials are on it, beat me to the draw and used it to put a bullet in my arm. I've been looking for him ever since. I'll keep the gun and when I catch up with him, I'll turn it loose on him and see how he likes being blasted to bits with his own gun. O-h, tell your friend back there," and he gestured with

22

the gun in the direction of the bar, "that I'll be back to see him later on and that he'd better have my money ready for me. If he doesn't, what he got just now won't begin to compare with what he'll get."

Clete Ainslee made two more stops along the street. Both places, Eph Turner's general store, and the bank, hadn't yet opened when he had tried their doors earlier. Eph's wife, Hannah, had just unlocked and opened the double doors to the store when Ainslee walked in. Hannah, who was about sixty-two, white-haired and motherly, greeted Ainslee with a smile and a bright "Good morning, young man."

"Morning, Ma'm. This your place?"

"You might say so," she replied with another smile and moved her glasses a little farther up on the bridge of her nose. "Actually, it's my husband's. But he's been bedridden for more than a year now. So I've taken over tending it. Now what would you like to have?"

"Ten dollars. That's what it's gonna cost you every week to do business here. I'll take the first week's payment now."

Hannah stared at him.

"Why, that's ridiculous! I never heard of such a thing. Now you get out of here before I call . . ."

He cuffed her across the mouth and sent her staggering backward. She collided heavily with the counter. She put her hand to her mouth; when she drew it back there was a smear of blood on her fingers. Her spectacles had been jarred loose and hung across her face from one ear. Disregarding them, she wheeled around and lunged across the counter at the youth who had stepped behind it and who had found and was opening the cash drawer. He brushed away her hands, slammed the drawer shut and pocketed the one bill it contained, a ten dollar bill, and came out from behind the counter.

"You . . . you young thief!" Hannah sputtered at him and she touched her lip again. "I'll have the law on you for this!"

"Yeah, you do that," he told her. "Now I'm gonna give you a tip, Grandma. The next time I come around for my money, that'll be a week from today, you have it ready for me, or that whack you just got, we-ll, you'll

23

get a lot worse. Now you remember that and we'll get along."

Jess Twombly who owned and managed the bank, and who doubled as cashier and bookkeeper, was seated at his desk just inside the open doorway thumbing through a ledger when Ainslee entered and came up to him.

"Y-es?" Twombly asked mechanically, taking his eyes from a column of figures on the first page and lifting his gaze.

Ainslee smiled at him and asked:

"Who runs this place?"

Twombly squared back in his chair.

"I do," he replied. "What can I do for you?"

"Beginning today, it's gonna cost you twenty-five dollars a week to do business here. I'm here to collect. So let's have it."

Ainslee's right arm jerked and Jess found himself staring into the muzzle of Len Shattuck's gun, it having replaced the gun in the youth's holster while his own Colt had been relegated to a position of secondary importance, shoved down out of the way inside the waistband of his levis.

"This . . . this is outrageous!" the banker blurted out.

"I don't think so," Ainslee said in reply. "I think it's cheap. Twenty-five bucks a week, or a hundred a month if you'd rather pay it that way, is letting you off easy in return for the protection I'm gonna give you."

"Protection?" Twombly echoed. "Protection against whom?"

Ainslee grinned broadly and said:

"Protection against somebody else who might come in here with the same idea as mine." He held out his left hand and snapped his fingers. "Come on, come on. Get it up. I haven't got all day."

The gun muzzle seemed to widen hungrily the longer Jess Twombly stared at it. He moved back in his chair, opened the middle drawer of his desk, took two tens and a five from a small, neat pile of bank notes and laid them on the desk.

"Hold it," Ainslee commanded. "Let's have the rest of it. The other seventy-five. That'll save me the trouble of having to come in here every week. Come on, let's have it."

24

Reluctantly Twombly handed over the additional seventy-five dollars. His visitor picked up the bills, folded them neatly and put them in his pocket. As he holstered his gun, he said:

"Nice doing business with a bank. Money's always clean and fresh, the kind I like. I'll see you again a month from today. So long."

He gave Twombly a nod and went out.

Retracing his steps upstreet to the saloon and smiling a little to himself as he marched along, Clete Ainslee did some mental addition of the various amounts of money that he had collected. In less than an hour's time the four dollars with which he had arrived in town had grown to nearly two hundred dollars and there was still more to be picked up, principally the saloonkeeper's fifty, to help swell the total. When he had completed the rounds he estimated that it would come to approximately three hundred dollars. He had never had that much money before. He was so delighted with himself and with his amazingly easily acquired wealth that he failed to notice that the stores he passed were shade drawn and that their doors were closed.

Humming to himself, he slanted across the walk to the saloon door. He did not think anything of it when he found it closed. When he tried the door and discovered that it was locked he was greatly surprised at first, and then annoyed. Frowning, he stepped up close to the window and hand-shading his eyes, peered in. It was shadowy inside, dark beyond the bar. He peered hard in an effort to see if anyone was in the place, but after a minute, satisfied that there was no one there, he stepped back. The saloonkeeper had probably gone home, he told himself, to lick and nurse his wounds. But if he thought for even a minute that that would have any softening or compromising effect on him, Ainslee, he had another thought coming, Ainslee assured himself. As a matter of fact, the effect it had on him would be just the reverse. Instead of fifty dollars a month, the levy would now come to seventy-five, and if there was any attempt to stall him off, it would go up to a hundred. That would teach the saloonkeeper the lesson that he appeared to need so badly.

Sauntering on, he stopped again shortly, this time a

little farther up the street, in front of the Macum, the town's only hotel, and eyed it critically. When he spied a weatherbeaten and faded signboard atop the building that read "Macum's Leading Hotel," he snorted scornfully, for what he could see was a drab, shabby, two-story structure with a sagging veranda fronting it. Two of the four windows on the upper floor were paneless, a further sign of the hotel's run-down condition. He was sure its accommodations would not only be limited but probably of the poorest kind. At that, he maintained, he couldn't afford to be too critical. He had to have a place in which to live, and if the Macum was the best he could find, he would have to accept it with good grace. Of course, he would insist upon having the best room in the house for himself, and he took it for granted that the proprietor wouldn't dare expect him to pay rent for it. Finally, he decided, in view of what he could see of the hotel and what he judged the owner's income to be, a five dollar a week levy would be the most he could reasonably impose upon the hotelkeeper.

He climbed three badly warped and rickety steps to the veranda, ignoring the floorboards that creaked and groaned underfoot, crossed it and entered the hotel. He found himself in a box-like lobby with a counter on one side and on the wall behind it a tier of ten crudely fashioned wooden mail boxes. There was nothing save a layer of dust in any of the boxes. Beyond the counter was a short flight of uncarpeted stairs.

"Hey!" he called out. "Anybody home?"

He had already taken note of a closed door a little past the counter. When there was no response to his call, he tried the door, found it was locked, and stood at the foot of the stairs listening for sounds of movement overhead. But the upper floor was quiet and with a snort of disgust he strode out. He looked annoyed when the floorboards squeaked dismally under his step, went down the three steps to the walk and halted there. The street was still deserted and still hushed. The mantle of silence that had suddenly draped itself over the town puzzled him and then irked him. More than anything else, the silence was so oppressive, it gave him an uneasy turn.

Suddenly aware that he was hungry, and remembering

that he hadn't had any breakfast, he crossed the street and headed for the lunchroom that he recalled having passed earlier. It was a small, dingy place with a short, narrow counter and some five or six stools lined up in front of it. A brief glance inside had made him decide that it wasn't worth bothering with. The emptiness inside of him began to make itself felt and he quickened his pace. He came up to the lunchroom shortly, stopped dead in his tracks, and glowered. He could see that there was no one inside. He tried the closed door anyway. It was locked. He gave vent to his disappointment by cursing and kicking the door. Turning, he sauntered out to the curb and stood there for a time, looking up the street and down. Macum had become a ghost town. Slowly he crossed to the opposite side and started upstreet again toward the hotel. He stopped instantly when he came abreast of the bank. The door was open and he could see the man from whom he had collected earlier still sitting at his desk. Ainslee went striding in. Jess Twombly lifted his eyes to him.

"Oh, it's you again," he said and eased back in his chair.

"Where's everybody?" Ainslee demanded of him. "And what's going on around here?"

"I beg your pardon?"

"Whole damned town's suddenly locked up tighter'n a drum," Ainslee went on heatedly. "Now you tell me what's going on and you'd better tell me quick."

His right arm jerked and he whipped out Shattuck's gun and held it almost in Twombly's face.

"Talk," Ainslee commanded.

"I'm afraid I can't tell you what I don't know," the banker said evenly. "As you can see I've been working on these ledgers all morning," and he pointed to a dozen or more account books that were piled up on the desk, "and I haven't been outside since I got here."

"Yeah, but somebody could have come in here and told you what . . ."

"No one's been in here this morning. No one but you."

"H'm," Ainslee said and drew back the gun. "Where can I get something to eat?"

"Only place I can suggest is the lunchroom across the street."

"It's closed," Ainslee said curtly. "Same's everything else is."

"Then again I'm afraid I can't help you."

"I'm not so sure about that. Where d'you eat?"

"I eat but two meals a day. Breakfast and supper. Doctor's orders."

"Yeah, but where d'you eat?" Ainslee pressed him.

"At home. That is, I live with my brother on his ranch eight miles from town."

Ainslee's eyes gleamed.

"I wouldn't be surprised if your brother has to set another place," he said.

Twombly shrugged.

"All right," he replied. "However, I think I should tell you this, though. My brother's son is there too."

"So what?"

"He's a United States marshal."

Ainslee looked hard at him.

"Forget it," he commanded, holstered the gun and stalked out.

FOUR

Stamping up the deserted street to the accompaniment of his thumping bootheels, Clete Asinlee's grim expression reflected his disappointment in the people of Macum for the way in which they had reacted to him and his demands. And the hollow, gnawing feeling in his stomach did not help matters any. Why, he kept asking himself, couldn't they have been more realistic about him? They were mature people and supposedly wise in the ways of the world. He wasn't the first man who had had the courage to impose his will upon others, and he knew he wouldn't be the last. Down through the ages there had always been those to whom others bowed down and paid tribute. So it wasn't something that he had originated. Admittedly, he hadn't expected everyone to obey him without some show of protest. So he had prepared himself for some opposition. But out-and-out defiance was something else again, something that he couldn't permit even though he hadn't wanted to hurt anyone. That was not the way to establish friendly relations and he had hoped to achieve them and thus make his stay in Macum a pleasant one. The three who had suffered at his hands, the saloonkeeper, the man who ran the hauling and freighting line, Smalley or Smallwood or whatever his name was, and the woman in the general store, if they had had the good sense that they should have had and if they had handed over the amount he had told them it would cost them weekly or monthly to go on doing business in Macum, he wouldn't have had any reason to manhandle any of them. The fact that he had had to resort to violence to convince them that he meant business was their fault entirely and he refused to accept any blame for it. We-ll, if closing down the town was their way of showing their resentment, he would show them that they couldn't dispose of him that easily. He would be patient and he would wait because sooner or later they would have to acknowledge his presence and reopen the town. Then they could make a fresh start with him, and understanding him, accept him, but without resentment. First off, though, he wished he could get something to eat.

Slowing his aimless striding and halting more or less mechanically in the entrance to an alley, he suddenly became aware of a savory fragrance of cooking that he couldn't withstand. Instantly he whirled around, seeking the source of it. At the far end of the alley was a shack, its door ajar, and he knew at once that the tantalizing smell was coming from there. As he hurried down the sloping length of the alley he dug in his pocket and fished out a couple of dollar bills and headed for the door of the shack. The closer he came to it, the more overpowering was the rich goodness of the cooking. He came up to the door and knocked on it and waited eagerly, impatiently. There was a step inside the shack, the door was yanked open wide and the full smell of the cooking flooded out and enveloped him. Instinctively he closed his eyes and breathed in deeply. When he opened them, he stared hard, for, poked out at him was a double-barreled shotgun that held on a line with his chest. His startled eyes lifted from the shotgun to the woman who was holding it on him, a hard-eyed, severely plain-featured and shabbily-clad woman of forty-five or so.

"Hello," he said with a bright smile. "I . . ."

"Yeah? You what?"

He held up the two dollar bills so that she could see them plainly and said with an even broader smile:

"I don't know what it is you're cooking in there . . ."

"Beef stew."

"Whatever it is, I know that nothing has ever smelled as good. There isn't any place in town where I can get a meal and I'm just about starved. Think I could get something to eat from you? I'm willing to pay for it, of course."

"Get out've here," she commanded, "or I'll blow you clear up the alley."

"You don't understand," he protested, and hauled out a five dollar bill and held it out to her too. "I don't want anything for nothing. I want to . . ."

30

"Get out've here," she repeated. "G'wan now . . . *git*."

"Look," he said in desperation. "I'll make it ten dollars. Is it a deal? And I'll even pay you in advance."

"You've got exactly one minute to hustle your miserable carcass up that alley and outta my sight," the woman told him. "If you aren't gone by then, you'll get it good. From both barrels."

"All right," he said, stepping back. "If that's the way you feel about it."

"That's exactly how I feel about it."

The woman moved into the open doorway with the shotgun still leveled at him. He turned around and started up the alley, looked back once over his shoulder. He saw the woman watching him, and quickened his pace. There was no question in his mind as to what she would do if he weren't gone in the brief time allowed him. As he neared the head of the alley, he pocketed the money.

"Nice people in this town," he muttered to himself. "The friendliest. And that old hag in there, I'll bet she doesn't remember the last time she had ten bucks all her own."

He emerged shortly from the alley and moved off and halted again just beyond it and lifted a scowling look up-street and then down. There was no one about. He sauntered out to the curb and stood there a little spread-legged with his thumbs hooked in his gunbelt. Focusing his gaze on the bank at the moment that Jess Twombly appeared in the open doorway, Ainslee hurried to join him.

"Now look, mister," he began darkly. "I . . ."

"It came to me right after you walked out that we've had four others in the past ten years with the same ideas as yours," the banker said, interrupting him. "But not one of the four lived to leave here. Three were hanged and the fourth one died right out there," and he pointed to a spot in the middle of the gutter, "with a dozen bullet holes in him. It wasn't the law that did it to him. It was the townspeople who finally rose up in their wrath and indignation who put an end to him and his tyranny. You might think about that before it's too late."

"Thanks for the advice," Ainslee retorted. "Only I don't want it."

Twombly shrugged.

"What's more," Ainslee continued, "I don't believe a word of that story."

"It's your privilege to believe or disbelieve."

"Damned right it is! If you thought you could throw a scare into me with that . . . that cock 'n bull yarn, it's no go because I don't scare easy."

"Clete Ainslee," Twombly said, pointing to the woven name above the youth's shirtpocket. "That your name?"

"What about it?"

"Nothing. Where do you come from, son?"

"None o' your damned business! And don't call me son!"

"Sorry," the banker said.

Ainslee leveled a hard look at him.

"Y'know," he said, "you could get on my nerves awf'lly easy. There's something smart alecky about you and I don't like that. So watch it, y'hear?"

Twombly turned to go back to his desk.

"Hold it!" Ainslee yelled after him. "I'm not finished with you!"

The banker stopped and looked back at him.

"Y-es?" he asked.

Ainslee crossed the threshold.

"I suppose you've got it all figured that the minute you get out to your brother's place you'll tell your nephew about me so he can come looking for me, right? You think I'm that stupid that I'm gonna let you go? No, mister, I'm not. So you can forget about going home today. Fact is you aren't going anywhere. You're gonna stay here and keep me company. Now what d'you think of that?"

"Whatever you say, Ainslee," Twombly answered with exasperating calm. "But if I fail to put in an appearance at home in time for supper, my nephew and very likely my brother too and probably some of his men will come looking for me. What then, my young friend?"

"Wouldn't you like to know!" Ainslee said sneeringly. He jerked out Shattuck's gun. "Come on. Let's go."

"All right," Twombly said. "I'm ready."

Ainslee looked at him oddly.

"Don't you want to put your stuff away and lock up before we go?" he asked.

"What for? Since everyone appears to be staying under cover . . ."

Ainslee did not press the matter.

"Let's go," he said simply.

With the gun back in his holster, but with his hand resting on the butt, he marched Jess Twombly up the street and into the hotel. The counter was still unmanned.

"Who runs this place?" Ainslee asked Twombly. "There wasn't anybody here before and there isn't now either. Helluva way to run a business, even one like this."

The banker made no response.

"Guess we'll just go on upstairs and find us a room," Ainslee told him, "and make ourselves comfortable. Go 'head."

With Ainslee following him, Twombly led the way up the stairs that creaked and groaned under them even more dismally than the front steps had but minutes before. Halting on the shadowy upper floor landing with closed doors on both sides of it, the banker waited for his captor, who came crowding up behind him, to decide which way to go.

"That way," the youth said, indicating the direction with a nod. "The front of the house. So I can see what's going on in the street."

Again Twombly led the way and again Ainslee trooped after him. The first room they entered had no windowpanes and at Ainslee's instance they backed out of it and tried another. Peering in over the banker's shoulder, Ainslee commented:

"Isn't much, is it? But this one's got glass in the windows and by and large I suppose it's about as good as anything else they've got here."

The whitewashed walls had yellowed in some spots and had turned brown in others. There were bits of plaster chipped out of them in some places while whole chunks had been gouged out in other places. Long, erratic cracks crisscrossed the ceiling. There was a single iron bedstead in the very middle of the room close to an uncovered window. A straightbacked chair stood on the other side of the window. A bureau with a fat and wobbly-based lamp on top of it filled one right-angling wall and a washstand that held a basin and a water pitcher occupied the opposite wall. Pushing past Twombly to the bed, Ainslee looked down at it and shook his head. There were no pillows, no blanket, and the sheet that covered the lumpy mattressed bed was badly

33

rumpled and soiled. Frowning, Ainslee ripped it off, balled it up and flung it across the room. It fluttered lifelessly to the floor in a far corner. He walked to the door and closed it and said over his shoulder:

"Can't even lock the door. No key." He came sauntering back from the door, caught up the chair and put it down in front of the window, swung it around and straddled it. Half-turning his head, he asked: "You gonna stand there all day? Why don't you sit on the bed?" Then just as he was about to square around again to the window, he asked, "What's your name?"

"Twombly. Jess Twombly."

"Sit down, Jess," Ainslee instructed him, and the banker, smiling a little at the boyish freedom with which the youth had addressed him by his first name, seated himself gingerly on the edge of the bed. But he kept eyeing the uncovered mattress rather suspiciously, ready to jump up at once if he saw anything crawl over it. He glanced at the turned Ainslee when he heard him say, "Boy, am I hungry!"

"Do you mind opening that window?" Twombly asked. "We can do with some air in here."

Half rising out of his chair, Ainslee leaned forward and ran up the window, and sank down again. The time passed slowly, almost reluctantly. Suddenly Ainslee twisted around and said:

"You were pretty mouthy before. S'matter with you now? Cat got your tongue?"

"N-o, just taking your advice and keeping quiet so that I don't get on your nerves."

"Yeah, but sitting there and staring at me so that I can feel your eyes boring into me is worse than having you run off at the mouth," Ainslee retorted. "Talk to me."

"What about?"

"Anything you like. 'Cept for your brother, you a loner like me?"

"A loner?" Twombly repeated.

"Yeah. Somebody who has to go it alone because he hasn't got anybody."

"I have two brothers and a sister."

"I haven't got anybody. Never knew my old man and my mother died when I was only about knee-high to a flat rock. From then on I lived with anybody who was willing to take

34

me in. Y'know something? There are damned few really good people in this lousy world. Most people are bastards. Mean and miserable clear through. I've been walloped and beaten so that I couldn't stand, and starved, too, by people who didn't care a whit that I was only a skinny little kid, and who tried to work me like I was a pack horse. But now I aim to make up for all that. The way I see it, the world owes me something, in fact, a helluva lot, and I aim to make it pay up."

Wisely, Twombly held his tongue.

"O-h, I've squared up pretty well with those good, good people who were so good to me. And some of them I even paid back double. Y'see, because I was always small and kinda puny, I had to find a way to make myself as big and strong as the biggest and the strongest. A gun did that for me. It's made me a giant. I learned how to handle it when I was about fourteen and from then on I practiced and practiced with it till now I'm as good and as fast as the best. And I'm making that pay off for me."

"There's something in the Bible, Clete, in the book of Matthew, that you'd do well to remember."

"Yeah?"

" 'All they who take the sword shall perish with the sword.' In your case, it will be your gun."

"So what? If that's the way it'll be, let it. If I get what I figure is due me and I get a chance to enjoy it even for only a little while, I won't care what happens."

"You're wrong, boy," the banker said. "Once you get what you want out of life, you'll want more than ever to live, and you will care."

Ainslee got to his feet, pushed the chair aside, and as Twombly followed him with his eyes, paced the floor. He stopped and squaring around to the banker, said:

"I started making the world pay up six months ago. Wanna know how many men I've killed already, counting those who got paid back for what they did to me, and those who tried to stop me from taking what I wanted? I'll tell you. Seven. And if I have to run it up to seventy-seven, it won't mean a thing to me. And you wanna know why? Because I don't care about anybody. I'm bitter, sure, and who has a better right? So I'm taking it out on everybody. And I'll go on doing that till I die."

FIVE

Having helped the brutally beaten and wobbly-legged Andy Horvath into the latter's tiny office at the rear of the saloon, Howie Dryden who hadn't wanted to become involved in something that didn't concern him and who had hoped to get out of Macum before there was trouble, found himself wallowing in it. Hurrying back to the bar, he returned with a bucket of water and a couple of towels that he found in a cabinet below the mirrored back wall. He proceeded to stop the bleeding, wash away the blood and patch up Horvath's wounds. Then still mindful of Ainslee's promise to return, he went scurrying out to the front door and locked it and closed the office door behind him too.

"What'd you do?" Horvath wanted to know. "You lock the street door?"

"Uh-huh," Dryden said.

"Think he's coming back, huh?"

"He said he was and I'm taking him at his word."

"That closet over there," the saloonkeeper said, pointing to a tall, wooden cabinet that stood in a corner, dwarfing everything else in his office. "You'll find two loaded rifles in the back. Be a good feller and haul th'm out."

Dryden had to fish around in the depths of the closet before he found the rifles hidden behind some clothes and some stacked up boxes. At Horvath's instance he propped them up against the wall near the door.

"That's it," the saloon man said. "Now we're all set for him and we can give it to him good."

Dryden suddenly flung a warning "Sh-h" at him and pressed his ear against the door. Instantly Horvath was on his feet. Snatching up the rifles he shoved one into Dryden's hands and stepped up next to him and asked low voiced:

"Somebody at the door?"

Dryden nodded.

"Think it was him?"

"Dunno. Whoever it was, he tried the door a couple o' times, then he went off."

"H'm," Horvath said thoughtfully. "Tell you what I'd like you to do, partner. Hey, by the way, what's your name?"

"Dryden. Howie Dryden."

"You're all right, Dryden, and I'm sure obliged to you."

"Aw, forget it."

"Nope. Andy Horvath never forgets anyone who does him a good turn and you sure did me one. And I aim to see to it that everybody in town knows it. You stuck by me and fixed me up and I won't forget that."

In all of Howie Dryden's forty-one years no one had ever thanked him or praised him for anything. He probably would not have admitted it, yet he knew he had never done anything to merit praise or thanks. A slow moving and slow thinking individual, awkward in the extreme because he was so ungainly, Horvath's thanks made him blush with embarrassment. Hastily he sought to cover up his embarrassment by asking:

"What'd you want me to do?"

"Huh? O-h, yeah! Like you to go round up the other storekeepers only on this side of the street though, and tell them to grab their rifles and hustle over here. When they're all here we'll figure out what to do about that murderin' young squirt."

"His name's Clete Ainslee," Dryden said. "Leastways, that's the name he's got sewed on his shirtpocket."

"Thanks for telling me. Now we'll know what to put on the marker when we bury him," Horvath said. "We've got a place ready for him alongside some others who came here with the same idea he's trying to pull on us. O-h, go out the back way, Dryden, and work your way through the yards. This Ainslee maverick is probably parading the street so there won't be any chance of him spotting you. All right?"

Twenty minutes later six grim-faced, rifle-armed storekeepers, two of them still wearing their ankle-length aprons, stood around in Horvath's office. A seventh man, big, brawny, sandy-haired Lars Thielesen, the local stableman, was the last to arrive. He reported that when he was watch-

37

ing from his hay loft window he had seen Ainslee herding Jess Twombly ahead of him into the hotel.

"I've got his horse stabled in my place," Thielesen added. "I was hoping that when he saw the town close down on him that he might decide to get his horse and go on his way. So I laid for him with that big manure shovel of mine. If he hadda showed up, I'd have busted him over the skull with it."

"Being that the hotel's an eye-sore and a rat hole," Horvath said, "if he didn't have Twombly with him, I'd say let's put the torch to it and burn him out."

Ed Small who like Horvath had been gun whipped and who was wearing a turban-like bandage wound around his battered head similar to the one that Dryden had fashioned for Horvath, said:

"I think it's just as well for us that we can't try to burn him out. He'd probably manage to make his way out. But I'm not so sure about Twombly, and I don't think we have the right to take a chance with Jess' life."

"On top o' that," another man, Kelsey Peters who ran the hardware store and lumber yard, added: "this Ainslee would come out shooting and chances are kill a couple of us before the others could get him. So we've got to come up with something that won't be so risky for us."

"All right, Ed, Kelsey," Horvath said. "Anybody got 'nything to suggest?" He looked from one to the other in the unevenly formed half-circle of men facing him. When no one offered anything, he lifted his eyes to Dryden who had backed off from the others and who was leaning against a side wall. "How about it, Dryden? If you've got an idea that we can use, let's hear it, huh?"

Those who had been standing backturned to Dryden turned and looked at him; those facing in his direction but simply glancing at him now focused their gaze and attention on him.

"We-ll," he began a little hesitantly, and he flushed again, embarrassed a second time for never before had anyone sought an idea from him or asked his opinion on anything. "I kinda think it figures that Ainslee grabbed this Twombly feller so he'd have something to trade with you, say Twombly's life for his, if he found himself in a bind that he couldn't get out've."

Some of the men showed no reaction to his words; others nodded and this so encouraged Dryden that he went on almost eagerly.

"Judging by what I've heard tell here, it looks to me like Ainslee's picked up enough dough around here already to give him a stake. So he oughta be satisfied to move on and try his luck somewhere's else. What he's got to do now is figure out when to make his move. I kinda think that come nightfall he'll herd Twombly down to the stable with him just in case he needs him. If he sees that the coast is clear, he'll probably dump Twombly, get up on his horse and head out."

Kelsey Peters looked disappointed.

"When you started talking, I thought you had something worth hearing. Now I'm not so sure," he said. "I don't like the idea of letting him get away. I think he's got something coming to him."

"I don't mean for you to let him get away," Dryden said.

"That's different," Peters said. "Then go on, partner. Let's hear what you've got in mind."

Dryden moistened his lips with the tip of his tongue.

"Like you know, this Ainslee's only pint size," he said shortly. "So it shouldn't take more'n two or three of you to do the trick. If the ones you pick slip into the stable say around sundown and hide away and stay outta sight, that'll set things up fine. When Ainslee comes in and looks around and doesn't see anybody, there won't be any call for him to get suspicious. He'll figure he's just about scared the britches offa everybody and that nobody's got the guts to do anything. His horse unsaddled, Mister Stableman?" he asked the towering Thielesen.

"Uh-huh," the latter answered.

"Good," Dryden said. "Then while his back is turned and he's busy saddling up, you three fellers step out on him, jump him and that'll be that."

"Hey," Peters said. "I think you've hit it, Mac, and right smack on the nose too."

"Yeah," Andy Horvath said. "I think he has too."

"Lars," Peters said, turning to Thielesen. "I'm willing to be one of the three to do the job. How about you?"

Thielesen grinned.

"It's my stable," he answered.

"What's that supposed to mean?" Ed Small asked.

"What d'you think it means?" Peters retorted and turned again to Dryden. "It's your idea, Mac. Want in on it with Lars and me?"

Before Dryden could answer, Horvath said:

"If anybody has the right to want in, Dryden has, and I say let him."

"Well, now," Small began and all eyes held on him. "After what that ornery young polecat did to you and me, Andy, I kinda thought we oughta have a crack at him. But if you're willing to step aside for this man," and he indicated Dryden with a jerk of his head, "then I guess I haven't any alternative but to go along with you."

"Just one minute now," Dryden said protestingly, holding up both of his hands. "While I want to see this Ainslee get what's coming to him, he doesn't mean anything special to me. Not like what he means to you people. So . . ."

"You've got a claim on him, Dryden," Horvath said, interrupting him. "Or have you forgotten?"

Dryden lifted puzzled eyes to him.

"How d'you mean, I've got a claim on him?"

"He took your gun off you, didn't he?"

"That's right, he did. But, heck . . ."

"Then you've got the right to take it back from him," the saloonkeeper said with finality. "Far as I'm concerned, it's all settled. You, Kelsey and Lars . . ."

"What about the rest of us?" someone asked.

"Yeah," still another storekeeper said. "What are we supposed to do? Just go home and stay put there?"

"Nope," Horvath told him. "Every one of us, in fact, every man in town oughta to be out tonight with his rifle covering the stable. There can always be a slip-up somewhere, y'know, in the best o' plans. And just to make sure that if there is that Ainslee doesn't get away, we'll cover the stable front and back, from the backyard and from the alley across the street, from the stable and from the roof of the building opposite it. But meanwhile I think you fellers," and he looked at Peters and Thielesen who were standing together and then at Dryden who was still backed against the wall, "oughta be talking things over so that when Ainslee walks into the stable the reception c'mmittee will be all set for him."

Seeking another chair, this one for Jess Twombly, Clete Ainslee found one in an adjoining room. When he brought it back with him, the banker, visibly relieved, accepted it with an appreciative nod and a murmured 'Thanks', and quickly transferred himself to it from the bed. The youth sauntered about aimlessly but returned every few minutes to the window for a quick look in the street below, and resumed his restless pacing.

"I hate this waiting around," he announced. "Whatever's gonna happen, I'd rather have it happen so I can get it over with." He stopped and half-turning to Twombly said: "Y'know, you weren't fooling me any when you didn't bother to put away those ledgers of yours. I knew you were purposely leaving them layin' around on your desk as a sign to whoever came looking for you that you weren't very far away."

Twombly's eyes didn't waiver when he met Ainslee's. But wisely again he made no attempt to answer. Ainslee went back to his chair shortly and straddled it as before. This time though he did not poke his head out the window.

"How long have you been living in this lousy town?" he asked without looking around at Twombly.

"O-h, a long, long time."

"Why? Have you always had such a good thing going for you here that you couldn't bring yourself to give it up?"

"N-o, not quite," the banker responded with a wry little smile. "It's just that I like it here."

Ainslee snorted.

"Dead as a cemetery," he said with a scornful twist of his lips, "and you like it here."

"It isn't always that way," Twombly said quietly.

"Mean it's only that way now on account o' me?"

Apparently still trying to avoid antagonizing the embittered youth, Twombly disregarded his question as though he hadn't heard it.

"When I first came here, I didn't like it at all," he told Ainslee in a reminiscing tone. "More than once I was on

41

the verge of pulling up stakes and going somewhere else. You see, Clete, in those days Macum was a pretty wide open town and all kinds of people, most of them undesirable, came here. But there were some good, decent people here also, and they prevailed upon me to stay. As time went on, more and more families came to Macum and soon the undesirables found themselves increasingly outnumbered and in a fast dwindling minority, and finally they moved on. The dance halls and the gambling casinos found they couldn't survive if they had to depend upon the townspeople for business. So they closed up and moved on too. The law had done a pretty fair job here prior to that. With the undesirables gone, it solidified its position in the community and it has retained its hold ever since."

"Where was the law and what did it do to stop those three you told me about from being strung up?" Ainslee demanded, twisting around.

"It just happened that each time one of those men with the same idea in mind that brought you here appeared in town and proceeded to set the idea in motion, we were without the services of a sheriff."

"G'wan," Ainslee retorted. "I don't believe that. It sounds to me like . . . like a put up job, like it was arranged that way."

"As I told you before, Clete, we're without a sheriff now," Twombly reminded him. "Do you think we arranged it that way for you too?"

"How do I know you didn't?"

"Just one thing more, Clete."

"Yeah?"

"Do you think those men were entitled to the protection of the law? Do you think you are?"

"I don't need anybody to protect me!" Ainslee shot back at Twombly. "This is all the protection I need," he went on a little wildly, slapping the gun in his holster. "Long's I've got it, I don't need the law or anything else because this is the law I live by!"

SIX

Howie Dryden was a coward. He knew it yet he would have disputed it with anyone who called him a coward. Of course he would have been careful to avoid making his denial too heated, and as he had done a couple of times when he had found himself within a word of a fight, he would have bought the man who was berating him, and practically challenging him, a drink, even two if he had thought it necessary in order to avoid the fight. And even though he disliked doing it he could recall the painful details of perhaps a dozen instances in his life beginning with his childhood when he had taken to panic-stricken flight to save himself from a beating. He tried desperately not to think of those times, tried to keep them a secret from himself as though he thought he could divide his memories and himself into two separate entities and keep each from learning too much about the other.

He had accompanied the Strangs in their ill-fated attempt to brace Len Shattuck only because he had had no alternative. Milt Strang had told him quite plainly that he would have to take a hand in it or he could draw his wages and go find himself another job. Because jobs were scarce, almost non-existent save for top hands, due to economic conditions, he had been forced to agree to participate in the bracing. But the moment the shooting had begun, he had panicked and he had thrown down his gun. His sudden overpowering lusting for Shattuck's blood was beyond his understanding. He had tried to explain it to himself. But the only explanation he had been able to come up with was that he had been carried away by the excitement of the moment. It had never happened to him before and he could not conceive of it happening to him again.

His purpose in acquiring Len Shattuck's gun would have been understood by anyone who really knew him. Unfortunately though he had never had any close friends. Everyone, he had told himself, knew Shattuck, and practically everyone had seen his gun at one time or another and would readily recognize it. But seeing it riding in Dryden's holster, he expected it would be taken for granted that he had bested Shattuck in a fight and that he had exercised the victor's right to appropriate the vanquished man's gun. So the sight of the gun would provide him with a mantle of immunity, for no one, he maintained, would be foolish enough to provoke a fight with a man who had downed a gunfighter of Shattuck's reputation.

Three times he had tried to bow out of participation in the plan that he had suggested for the capture of Clete Ainslee. But neither Andy Horvath nor Kelsey Peters who had decided to stay on in the saloonkeeper's office after Thielesen and the others had gone would hear of it. Finally Dryden decided that he wouldn't say any more about it. If they thought as he hoped they did that his desire to withdraw was simply due to his unwillingness to hurt the feelings of someone else who had more of a grievance against Ainslee than he had, he wanted them to go on thinking that. And since there was no way out of it for him, he would pretend to be quite satisfied and willing to go through with it. But he assured himself he would see to it that he kept out of harm's way while Peters and the brawny Thielesen did the actual overpowering of the youth. When it was over, he would reclaim his gun and he would be quite content. Of course if Ainslee decided to defy the townspeople and stay on no one could blame that on him. He could pretend to be as sorry about that as the next man. But at the same time he'd decline to take a hand in any other plans to capture or dispose of the unwanted Ainslee.

The three men sat around Horvath's office talking a bit but actually whiling away the time. Finally the afternoon was gone. Peters got up and stretched himself, caught up his rifle, looked at Dryden and said:

"Time for us to go, partner. Gets dark out here all uva sudden, y'know, sometimes even before we expect it. So I think we oughta be getting ourselves down to the stable and setting things up."

Dryden nodded and climbed to his feet.

"Good luck, you fellers," Horvath said.

"Yeah, sure," Peters acknowledged with a wry grin and led the way out.

Trudging along at his heels, Dryden followed him through the yards to the back door of the stable. But as they came up to it and Peters raised his hand to rap on it, the door opened and Lars Thielesen peered out at them, grunted, backed with the door, held it wide for them, and closed it after them.

"Been waiting for you," he told them simply but low voiced. "Got a tiny light burning inside. Don't want him to get suspicious and maybe even shy off if there isn't some kind o' light showing."

"Uh-huh," Peters said.

"Come on," Thielesen said, and, turning on his heel, led them inside. There were stalls on both sides of the stable and most of them were occupied. A couple of the horses greeted them with a whinny while another snorted, pawed the floor of his stall with his hoof and slapped the wooden side of his cubicle with his tail. Thielesen stopped abruptly in front of one stall and told Dryden: "That's your horse in there. Found him standing across the street right after I'd heard about that Ainslee squirt. Afraid there might be some shooting and that he might get caught in between, so I brought him in here. That mare next to him is Ainslee's. That's his saddle over there," he added and pointed to a saddle that was straddling a wooden horse. "Got it right handy for him."

"Yeah," was Kelsey Peters' comment.

Bits of harness hung from wall pegs. There were wagon wheels, new ones as well as some in need of repair, propped up against the walls. Wire banded bales of hay were stacked up beyond them to varying heights, some of them reaching almost to the ceiling. The body of a light wagon was upended and catercornered two right-angling walls. Peters peered behind the wagon body and squeezed himself in.

"Hey," he said shortly in a muffled voice. "This is all right. Fact is, it's perfect."

"Yeah, but d'you think you'll be able to bust outta there in a hurry and without makin' a to-do about it?" Thielesen wanted to know.

"O-h, sure!"

"All right, Kel, if you say so. Only you wanna remember that when the time comes to jump him we're gonna have to move fast. So fast that he won't get the chance to go for his gun."

"I'll bet you I beat you to him."

Thielesen laughed lightly.

"You'll try, I know that," he said. "And I hope you make it."

"I'll make it, all right," Peters assured him, and added: "And I hope you make it."

"How about me on top o' those bales o' hay?" Dryden asked the big stableman, pointing to a stack-up that reared itself ceilingward at least fifteen feet above the hay and oat strewn floor. "If you give me a boost up . . ."

"Yeah, sure," Thielesen said with a nod. He helped Dryden climb up. Then he backed off a couple of steps, looked up at him and said: "If you kinda flatten out up there . . ."

Dryden sprawled out on his stomach and raising up the barest bit peered down over the edge of the top bale.

"That's it," the stableman told him.

"Where'll you be, Lars?" Peters asked, again in a muffled voice.

"I'll be around, all right, Kel. And chances are closer to him than you or Dryden. Although Dryden'll be right above him and all he'll have to . . ."

"Hey, Dryden," Peters called out. "Don't hog the whole thing now. Be a good feller and leave some of Ainslee for us."

Dryden did not answer him. He could have told Peters that neither Thielesen nor he had anything to fear from him because he intended to leave all of Ainslee to them. He watched Thielesen back his horse out of his stall and he looked on wonderingly. But then the stableman maneuvered the animal into another stall. His eyes held on Thielesen as he came trudging back, crunching hay and oats underfoot. The latter dragged two bales across the floor and into the vacated stall and with a heave of his body and his muscular arms hoisted one on top of the other. Dryden's gaze shifted away from him briefly to the doorway that opened on the alley down which Ainslee would have to come. It was dark outside. When he looked again in the direction of the stall there was no sign o

Thielesen. Dryden took it for granted that the stableman had taken up his post behind the two bales.

While he had been aware of the dim light, he hadn't given it any more than the barest mechanical glance. Now, though, his attention was attracted to it. The lamp hung from a ceiling rafter at the end of a short cut of tarnished chain. The turned down light flickered a couple of times when a sudden gust of air came swirling in from the alley. But then it steadied and burned evenly, casting off a small circle of yellowish, eerie light on the floor below it, leaving the area immediately beyond the circle in shadows, the far reaches and the corners of the stable in gloomy darkness.

If Ainslee were to bear out his prediction that he would abandon Macum to the townspeople who resented him, Dryden hoped he would appear soon. Because of the limited space atop the baled up hay, Dryden lay in a most uncomfortable and cramped position with his bony knees drawn up and nudging his stomach and his equally bony backside pressed hard against the unyielding wall behind him. It was admittedly uncomfortable. Despite that, he would manage somehow, he told himself, if he wasn't forced to stay in that position too long. But if Ainslee delayed his departure till far later on into the night or into the early dawn . . .

The time passed slowly, painfully too, for Howie Dryden. Frowning, he moved himself a bit in an effort to ease himself. But it didn't help very much. There simply wasn't enough room for his gangling, angular body.

"O-h, why'n blazes doesn't he come on down here and get it over with?" he demanded crossly of himself.

Still seeking a more comfortable position for his aching and protesting body, he kept shifting himself one way and then another. Finally though he lay still again. But suddenly he stiffened and listened intently. He had heard something, something that he could not readily identify. It wasn't anything like the usual night sounds. He heard it again, stronger this time and he held his breath as he listened. Then he recognized it. It dissolved into slow, cautious footsteps, and they were coming down the alley. His heart began to beat furiously. It thumped in his chest and the pounding filled his ears. For an instant he was on the verge of panicking. But he fought to control himself and he succeeded. After all, he asked himself, what did he have to fear? He was only a bystander, a looker on who had no intention of taking a hand in what was soon to happen. If anyone had anything to be concerned about it was his two hidden companions. Reassured and calmer, he burrowed low atop the bale and focused his wide eyes on the doorway. The approaching bootsteps came steadily closer. Dryden's heart beat a little faster. He shot a quick, anxious look at the upended wagon body and then at the stall with the stacked up bales of hay and sought some sort of sign that would indicate to him that both Peters and Thielesen were aware that someone was coming down the alley. But there was no sign from either man and Dryden's fears began to return. He shrank back as far as the wall permitted and held his breath lest he betray himself to Ainslee.

Then, suddenly, there was a man framed in the open doorway, a hatless, middle-aged man whom Dryden knew he had never seen before. And behind him and peering in over the stranger's sloping shoulder was a second man whom Dryden recognized at once. It was Clete Ainslee. Dryden, eyeing the first man, wondered who he was. Suddenly it came to him that he was Jess Twombly, the man whom Thielesen had reported having seen Ainslee herding ahead of him into the hotel. When Ainslee nudged him, Twombly took a couple of steps into the stable and halted again, turned after a moment and said:

"I think it's quite safe for you, Clete. Doesn't seem to be anyone around."

"Sh-h," the youth cautioned him. "Keep it low, Jess." He stepped around the banker and then Dryden saw that he had a gun in his hand. He wondered if it was Shattuck's. Ainslee lifted his gaze and ranged a quick look around the stable. He tiptoed over to the first stall and peered in, and obviously recognizing his mare, proceeded to back her out. When his searching eyes lit on his saddle straddling the wooden horse, he holstered his gun, lifted the saddle and slapped it on the mare's back. Suddenly there was movement behind the upended wagon body and with a sweep of his hand, Ainslee brushed Twombly back and out of the way. As the youth whipped out his gun and snapped it up and leveled it at the wagon body, the careening banker, stumbling clumsily, tripped over his own feet and crashed headlong into the bales of hay on top of which Howie Dryden was perched. The bales swayed to and fro and finally caromed off the wall, and the hapless Dryden, unable to do anything to save himself, was catapulted through space with his long arms outflung. He soared over Twombly's and came plummeting down squarely on top of the backturned Ainslee and practically ground him into the stable floor beneath him.

Clete Ainslee's capture was completed by Lars Thielesen and Kelsey Peters who pounced upon the youth who somehow had managed to partially free himself of Dryden. While the big stableman held him pinned to the floor, Peters disarmed him and used Ainslee's belt to lash his wrists together behind him. Then Thielesen climbed off him and hauled the somewhat dazed and rubbery-legged youth to his feet. Bleeding from his mashed nose, his tailor-made shirt half torn off him and his form-fitting levis showing the effect of too close contact with the stable floor, Ainslee was left in Thielesen's custody while Peters ran to the door and yelled something. There was an immediate response to his yell. A horde of rifle-armed storekeepers and townsmen with white turbaned Andy Horvath leading them came swarming into the alley. Some of the men had lighted lanterns with them and they held them high. Someone produced a rope and it was quickly noosed around Ainslee's neck. Peters and Thielesen surrendered their captive to the others who promptly surrounded him and hustled him streetward. As they emerged with him from the alley, there were running bootsteps and a tall, rangy man followed by a handful of panting and wheezing townsmen came dashing up and skidded to a halt in front of Horvath, Ainslee and the other men. There was a shiny, light-reflecting badge pinned to the flap of the tall man's shirtpocket.

"O-h," somebody said. "It's Ed Twombly."

"H'llo, Marshal," another man said.

The newcomer held up his hands.

"All right, boys," he said amiably. But there was no mistaking the ring of authority in his voice despite his obvious effort to play it down. "Hold it now. This is as far as you go. The law has first claim to your prisoner. So take the rope off him."

"Aw, come on now, Ed," Horvath protested. "You don't know what this young bastid's been doing around here."

"That's right, Marshal," someone said.

"I know what he's been up to," was the reply. "But that isn't all I know about him. For instance, that there's a want out for him for murder. And two different states would like it an awful lot if they could get their hands on him. What I didn't know till just a while ago was that he was here in Macum. Word I had was that he had headed north. Go on now, take the rope off him. The law will supply its own. O-h, any of you know where my uncle is?"

"He's inside," Kelsey Peters answered from where he was standing in the alley and he indicated the stable with a nod. "Got himself spilled on the floor. But he wasn't hurt any. Dustin' himself off last I saw of him."

"Uh-huh. Where's your horse, Ainslee?" Ed Twombly asked.

"In the stable," was the youth's curt reply.

"Partner," the marshal called to Peters. "You mind telling my uncle I'm here and that I'm waiting for him? And while you're at it, I'd sure be obliged if you'd have the stableman bring this young feller's horse out here."

"Right, Marshal," Peters answered, turned and marched down the alley.

Ed Twombly stepped up to Clete Ainslee, and towering over him, loosened the noose around his neck and lifted it off and tossed the rope into Andy Horvath's hands. Ainslee turned himself around so that the marshal could see his bound wrists and asked over his shoulder:

"How about this?"

"All right, how about it?"

"How will I ride with my hands tied behind me?"

"That'll be up to you."

"Suppose I fall off?"

"You'll get up and climb on again."

"By myself?"

"Uh-huh."

"And if I can't make it by myself?"

"Then you'll walk."

Some of the men flanking Ainslee grinned, others laughed. The youth turned and glared at them. Ed Twombly shouldered him aside as a path opened for him and he started down the alley. But he stopped almost at once when hoofs thumped on the hard-packed ground in the alley. Lars Thielesen, leading Ainslee's saddled horse, came up the sloping ground followed by Jess Twombly and Kelsey Peters. Another man, Howie Dryden, plodded after them, slowly though and at something of a distance. In his holster was a gun, Len Shattuck's. He had reclaimed it and he was satisfied. He would have been even more satisfied had he been able to saddle up and go on his way. But Peters and Thielesen wouldn't hear of it. They had refused to accept his story that he hadn't really leaped down upon Ainslee and they laughed off his explanation that it had come about as a result of a freak accident. Jess Twombly remembered bumping into the piled up bales of hay. But he was certain that he hadn't bumped them hard enough to dislodge Dryden.

"That's right," Thielesen had said with a nod. "Just happened to poke my head out at that moment and I saw you come diving down offa those bales and I know blamed well you couldn't've if you had been knocked off th'm like you want us to think."

"Why d'you hafta be so doggoned modest, huh?" Peters had demanded of Dryden.

"If that's the way he wants to be, let him," Thielesen had said. "I know what I saw and I saw him flatten Ainslee so that all we had to do was finish the job on that young bastid. So like it or not, Dryden, you're getting all the credit for fixing Ainslee and if anybody wants to argue about it, Kel and I'll be right glad to accommodate 'em."

"Right," Peters had concluded with an agreeing nod.

But because he knew he was not deserving of any praise for his participation in the capture of Clete Ainslee, he felt uncomfortable about it and it showed in his step. Actually his hesitancy was a reflection of a fear that he might be found out later on, and that, he knew, he wouldn't be able to face.

SEVEN

The Twomblys with Clete Ainslee in tow had gone, Marshal Ed having announced his intention of dropping off his uncle at home and then riding on with his prisoner to the county seat. There Ainslee would be handed over to the authorities who would decide what was to be done with him.

Andy Horvath had reopened his saloon, and with its lamps turned up to the fullest, light streamed out into the street and burned happily rather than defiantly against the night, for this was an occasion. Just about every man in town was there. That included the storekeepers who were in a festive mood because the money that they had been forced to contribute to Ainslee had been returned to them. Horvath's announcement that the drinks were on the house made the occasion a real celebration. Despite his battered head and the fact that movement and the din of voices must have made it throb, he insisted upon taking his customary place behind the bar. He poured generously and with both hands. Howie Dryden, flanked by Kelsey Peters and Lars Thielesen, looked uncomfortably suspicious when Peters suddenly caught up a chair, swung it around and climbed up on it and yelled for silence. It took half a minute or so for the hum of voices to die down.

"I wanna propose a toast. So if anybody has an empty glass in his fist it's his own fault and not Andy's. So get your glasses filled up," he commanded. There was a converging rush on the bar. When Peters was satisfied that every man had a drink, he said: "I wanna propose a toast to a man who was a stranger to us this morning but who isn't one any longer. Macum owes this man a lot. 'Course being modest, he insists he didn't do anything. We know different. He cooked up the plan for us to get that young squirt Ainslee and on top o' that took the lead and showed us the kind o' guts he has by jumping Ainslee all by himself. So let's drink to him, friends. Let's drink to Howie Dryden!"

"Wait a minute!" Thielesen yelled and all glasses stopped in mid-air. "An idea's just come to me and I think you oughta hear it. We need a sheriff. How about pinning the star on Dryden, huh? What do you say, men?"

There was an immediate roar of approval and townsmen and storekeepers swarmed around Dryden. Some of them patted him on the back while others like Thielesen, Peters and Horvath insisted upon pumping his hand. When things had quieted down a bit, a man who had moved in next to Dryden and who had noticed Shattuck's gun in his holster and obviously recognized it, nudged him and said:

"Good thing you're not the superstitious kind like me, partner. I wouldn't want to own a killer's gun. I'd be afraid there'd be some kind of curse on it."

Dryden leveled a hard look at the man.

"I hail from Kansas," the latter continued, hunching over the bar and crossing his arms on the lip. "Lawman I used to know right well back home had been doing all right for himself for years with his own gun. He got into a fuss with some hired gunny who had made something of a reputation for himself for being real fast. Well, sir, Sloat, this lawman friend o' mine, beat him to the draw when the gunny went for his gun, and killed him. He kept the gunny's Colt for himself and sold his own. But the very next day, some feller who didn't know any more about a gun 'cept which end of it to hold got himself likkered up and because he'd once had a run-in with Sloat went gunning for him. Now get this, partner. He outshot ol' Tom and killed him. Sloat fired at him three times without hitting him once while this other feller shot twice and hit him dead center both times. That's the story, partner. Maybe it proves something, maybe it doesn't. But like I said before . . ."

Dryden didn't wait for him to finish. He stepped back from the bar, turned on his heel, and left the man staring after him wonderingly, and stalked out. He wasn't concerned about Shattuck's gun being cursed. That was ridiculous. What was troubling him was the job with which he

54

had just been saddled. A lawman's job was the last thing he wanted. A man who had turned tail and who had taken to frightened flight in order to avoid a fight wasn't the kind of man to wear a star. Dryden knew he had to get out of Macum before it was too late. If he delayed, the very first man who questioned his authority would show him up for what he really was.

Minutes later he was in the stable. He saddled his horse, strapped on his blanket roll, climbed up astride the animal, rode him out of the stable and up the alley. In order to avoid passing the saloon and attracting attention to himself, he rode upstreet and away from it. When he had left Macum behind him, he drummed eastward for about a quarter of a mile, wheeled his horse and circling wide around the town, headed westward.

It was shortly after nine o'clock the next morning when Howie Dryden, tired and saddle-stiff, rode into the town of Kittings, some thirty-odd miles northwestward of Macum. Save for four saddle horses that were bunched together but not tied up at a hitchrail midway down the street, there was no one about and no sign of activity anywhere. Dryden looked surprised. A large signboard that jutted out from the flat roof of a building just a couple of diagonal steps beyond the hitchrail and the horses caught his eye. It bore a single word . . . BANK. The signboard extended out to the curb where a white-painted post rose up to meet and help support it. As he rode in closer to the curb, two rifle-armed men suddenly stepped out of an alley between the bank and the building next to it and held their rifles on Dryden. Startled, he pulled his horse to an immediate stop.

"All right, Mac," one man commanded. "Stay put there and unbuckle your gun belt and let it drop."

Dryden's heart began to pound. But in his eagerness to obey he fumbled nervously and experienced some difficulty unbuckling his belt. Finally though it dropped in the gutter at his horse's feet. The animal, as tired-looking as his rider, looked down at it wonderingly and watched the dust boil up around it and slowly settle again, blinked and closed his eyes and stood headbowed. One of the riflemen stepped down into the gutter and picked up Dryden's belt, yanked the gun out of the holster and tossed the belt away. He was about to shove the gun down inside the waistband of his levis when something about it stayed his hand. He examined the gun closely, turning it over in his hand and glanced at the butt, suddenly looked up at his companion and called to him:

"Hey, Marty, y'know what I've got here?"

"Yeah, what?"

"Len Shattuck's gun. You know, the one with all the fancy fixings. Got his initials on it too. So I know it's his all right. Now what d'you know about that?"

Obviously the man named Marty was not overly impressed.

"Climb down, Mac," he said to Dryden. "Keep an eye on him, Phil, while I go see what's keeping them so long."

Just as he turned toward the bank, there was a roar of gunfire inside the building, and two men, each with a gun in one hand and a canvas bag clutched in the other hand, backed out, whirled around and ran toward the bunched-together horses. Marty and Phil followed them. Phil took the time to shove his rifle into his saddleboot before he swung up on his horse. His companions, already mounted, lashed their horses and sent them bounding away. Phil, with Shattuck's gun in his hand, rode after them. A Colt roared a couple of times and one of the bag-clutching horsemen sagged and almost fell out of his saddle. But he managed somehow to keep his seat and rode on. A rifle cracked spitefully and Phil was hit. He swayed and toppled off his horse and crashed heavily in the gutter and slumped over on his face. His mount with the empty stirrups swinging wildly and thumping against his sides snorted and galloped after the others, and with them rounded the far corner in full pounding flight and disappeared from view. Dryden, rooted to the spot on which he stood, was suddenly aware of men's heads poked out at him from alleys and half-opened doors on both sides of the street.

A slight, stoop-shouldered man who limped badly and who had a rifle slung under his right arm came out of a building, hobbled out to the curb and stepping down into the gutter came together with another man who emerged from an alley. They talked briefly, turned and bent over Phil, pushed him over on his back and peered hard at him for a moment or two. Then straightening up they came up the street toward Dryden. The rifleman, an old timer with a pinched and weatherbeaten face and gnarled hands, glanced at Dryden as he neared him, stepped up on the planked walk and hobbled into the bank. The other man, a lean, greying man who wore a star pinned to his vest, had a Colt gripped in his right hand, and in his left, Shattuck's gun. He halted squarely in front of Dryden.

"I saw him," he said, and, half-turning, nodded in the direction of the fallen Phil, "take this gun outta your holster." He held out the gun to Dryden who nodded and took it from him. "I've seen that gun so many times before, I'd know it anywhere. Len Shattuck wasn't the kind to give it away or lose it. That gun was part of him. D'you mind telling me how you got it?"

"Shattuck's dead," Dryden answered simply, and before he could stop himself, he blurted out: "I killed him."

The lawman stared at him.

"We-ll, I'll be damned!" he said after a brief silence and a far closer study of the lanky and awkward looking Dryden. "Len Shattuck was just about the fastest gun I ever saw. And you say you killed him. If you don't mind me saying this, Mister, you don't look like the killer kind to me. Fact is, I don't think I've ever seen anybody who looked less like a killer than . . ."

Dryden's frown stopped the sheriff, and made him wonder if he shouldn't have been more cautious and less openly skeptical about the stranger's claim. It was one thing to entertain doubts and even disbeliefs. It was something else again to voice them when one had no way of knowing for certain that what he had been told was true or untrue. And to be frankly skeptical of a stranger who appeared wearing Shattuck's gun and thereby antagonize him was foolish. So till he knew better he would have to accept the stranger's claim and go along with it. Hastily then he sought to make amends.

"Guess when you get right down to it, Mister, no man ever looks like what he really is or what he's capable of doing," he said with what he must have thought was a

57

disarming smile. "You must be a real gun slick to've taken some one like Len Shattuck."

Dryden did not answer. He turned away, picked up his belt, slapped it against his leg in an effort to rid it of the dust that had boiled up around it, holstered the gun and buckled on the belt. A young woman who was prettier than any that he had ever seen before emerged from the bank. He stared at her with wide eyes, open-mouthed too, as she came swishing across the walk and out to the curb. He got a breath of the rich, heady cologne she was wearing and he inhaled deeply. When she glanced at him, he blushed and swallowed hard. She leveled her full gaze at the sheriff.

"Well?" she demanded wrathfully of him. Dryden heard her voice, but it sounded far off even though she was standing within touching distance of him. His eyes were devouring her hungrily. The curve of her lips, dew-moist and provocative, the soft sweep of her throat, the silky smoothness of her skin, her delicately chiseled features, her brilliant, flashing eyes that were green and grey and blue all at the same time, and her auburn hair that the morning sun touched with gold, held him in fascination. But if she felt his eyes on her, she gave no sign of it. Lost in her beauty, he found himself wondering what it would be like to hold her in his arms, what it would be like to feel her lips against his, wondered too what her kiss would taste like. "Well, Sheriff?" he heard her ask. This time though her voice was stronger and clearer, as he would have expected it to be from hardly more than a foot or two away. "What are you waiting for? Those men got away with nine hundred dollars of my money. Why haven't you gone after them?"

"By myself?" the lawman countered calmly. Shaking his head, he said: "Not me, lady. I'm not that much tired of living. Twice when I asked you to let me take on a deputy, you and your hand-picked town council turned me down cold. When I told you I'd heard that the Shannon gang had been seen around here and that they might be fixin' to pay you another visit, you pooh-poohed the idea and said they wouldn't dare try to hold you up again. When I tried to get some men together so we'd be set for the Shannons if they did hit Kittings again, you killed that.

58

Only one who was willing to give me a hand was old Davy Harper. He got that maverick layin' over there," and half-turning, he jerked his head in Phil's direction. "I put a bullet in one of the three who got away."

"Yes, but . . ."

The sheriff stopped her with a gesture.

"I'm not finished yet," he told her curtly. "When I set out to speak my piece, I don't let anybody stop me. And I've been saving up what I've got to say for a long time. I've had just about enough of you, your high an' mighty ways, of Kittings and the people of Kittings who don't even own their own souls because you own them and just about everything else worth owning in this lousy town. So while I've still got some respect for myself left, I'm quitting." He unpinned his star and pushed it into her hand. Gesturing again, he said: "G'wan, pin it on yourself. You bought it, so you've got a better right to wear it than anybody else. Now you can go round up a posse and go after those Shannons." He stepped back from her, stopped and looked at Dryden and then again at her and said: "This feller says he killed Len Shattuck. At first, I couldn't bring myself to believe it. But all uva sudden I do. Because that's Shattuck's gun he's wearing and I know blamed well it wouldn't be if Shattuck was still alive. Maybe you can sweet-talk him into taking on the job of being your sheriff. As for you, Mister," and he turned again to Dryden and said: "If she does, I'm sorry for you. If ever there was a bitch, she's it."

He turned on his heel and stalked away. The woman's burning eyes followed him.

"If I were a man, I'd kill him," Dryden heard her say and he looked at her. "Why I've put up with him all these years, I'll never know. I should have got rid of him a long time ago." But then the burning went out of her eyes. She smiled and said: "I'm Marie Norton. What's your name?"

"Huh? Oh! Name's Dryden, Ma'm. Howie Dryden."

A man came out of the bank, a well built, good looking man of about thirty-five or so, clad in expertly fitted and tailored clothes. Marie Norton turned when she heard his step, and beckoned, and he came at once to her side. He looked questioningly at her, then at Dryden:

"Mr. Dryden," she said, again with a smile, this one parting her lips and revealing perfectly formed even white teeth that fairly shone, "I'd like you to know my attorney and friend, Richard Quinlan. Richard, Mr. Dryden."

The two men shook hands, Quinlan pumping Dryden's hand warmly and vigorously.

"Happy to know you, Mr. Dryden," the attorney told him.

Dryden murmured a response.

"Richard," the Norton woman said, "I've news for you. That despicable Len Shattuck is dead and we can thank Mr. Dryden for ridding us of him."

"Society as a whole is indebted to you, Mr. Dryden," Quinlan said, "for the service you've rendered it." Then turning away from Dryden for a moment, he said: "Marie, must we stand out here and talk when your private office is so much more comfortable? I'd like to get better acquainted with our good friend here, and I'm sure you would too."

"Of course," she answered.

Flashing another but even warmer smile this time at Dryden, she slipped her arm through his, and with Richard Quinlan flanking him on the other side, Dryden was led into the bank.

EIGHT

Howie Dryden who had never known anything better in his adult life than the crude and makeshift confines of a bunkhouse or a line rider's cabin found himself in a breathtakingly new world when he was ushered into Marie Norton's private office. A rich, thickly piled rug that covered the floor from wall to wall absorbed and cushioned his hesitant step. A brocaded drapery that hung from within inches of the ceiling and touched the floor and ran from one right-angling wall to the other shut out the daylight and the outside world. Tall, graceful, slender stemmed crystal lamps with silk shades furnished the light. One of them stood on a small square table between two deeply recessed, tapestry-covered armchairs that were backgrounded by the drapery. The other lamp occupied a corner spot atop a highly polished and finely carved desk that graced the middle of the room. A high-backed leather-covered armchair stood majestically behind the desk. A sofa filled one side wall; opposite it was a highboy, double-doored with bronze fittings and handles. The wood was the same in all the pieces of furniture, the style, the legs and the carving identical throughout too. There were framed paintings on the walls, but they seemed to make little impression on Dryden whose appreciation of art was so limited as to be practically non-existant. Hence he did little more than glance at them and promptly look away again.

"Those paintings are the work of the best craftsmen in Europe," Quinlan said at his elbow.

"Uh-huh," Dryden said. But the furnishings obviously impressed him greatly for he added: "Sure got some place here. And that curtain," he said, pointing to the drapery, "that's nice."

Quinlan coughed behind his hand, took Dryden's hat from him and laid it on the sofa, nodded in the direction

61

of the armchairs and watched Dryden cross to the one nearest him, turn and carefully ease himself down in it. But he did not square back in it. Instead he sat rather gingerly on the very edge of it. Marie, who had halted in the open doorway, smiled and said:

"I'll leave you two to indulge yourselves in your men's talk without benefit of an audience." Half-turned to go, she stopped and looked back over her shoulder. "The liquor cabinet's unlocked, Richard. Please help yourself."

"Thank you, my dear," Quinlan responded and closed the door after her. Backed against it and meeting Dryden's eyes, he said: "There goes a wonderful woman, Dryden. Unfortunately though, a very unhappy one."

Dryden's surprise mirrored his surprise.

"I think I know what's going through your mind," the lawyer said as he came away from the door, walked to the highboy, opened it and drew back the doors. "You can't understand how anyone who has so much can be so unhappy." He brought out a silver-trimmed bottle and put it on the desk and followed it with two whiskey glasses, half-filled them and handed one to Dryden. Raising his glass, he said: "To us, Dryden, and to our friendship. May we and it endure."

Dryden grunted a throaty, indistinct and doubtless inadequate response. They drained their glasses. The liquor had a rich mellow smoothness that was unlike any that Dryden had ever tasted before. He licked his lips with the tip of his tongue.

"That's good stuff," he said. Quinlan smiled and refilled their glasses. Suddenly uneasy and suspecting something because no one had ever shown any particular interest in him and because the lawyer's treatment of him was a new experience for him, he blurted out: "Now look, Mr. Quinlan, if you're being so nice to me because you're fixin' to offer me the sheriff's job . . ."

"Nothing could be further from my mind," Quinlan said quickly, interrupting him. "That isn't the kind of job for you. A man like you, you're made for bigger and better things."

Dryden looked relieved. He showed it by squirming back in his chair.

"Drink up," Quinlan said.

Again they drained their glasses and this time Dryden smacked his lips.

"That's the best whiskey I've ever drunk," he said.

Quinlan put the bottle on the little table between the two armchairs, then glass in hand he seated himself in the vacant chair. He put his glass on the table too.

"Marie was just eighteen when her father, Jim Norton, died," he began. "He left her this bank and quite a lot of money. In his will he had named his closest friend, John Haislip, a man his own age, executor of his estate. But he had worded his will in such a way that Marie could not touch a single dollar of her inheritance without Haislip's approval. On top of that he neglected to specify any age for Marie to have her inheritance turned over to her. As you can understand, when a young girl who has always led a sheltered life suddenly finds herself alone in the world, she panics. When she ran to Haislip, he comforted her all right, made her think she would never be safe anywhere but with him."

"Talked her into marryin' him, huh?"

Quinlan nodded grimly.

"That's right. But once they were married, he became a different man. There wasn't a day in their three years together that he didn't beat or mistreat her. When she couldn't stand it any longer, she left him."

"Man has to be pretty low to do something like that. I mean, beat a woman."

"Haislip's the lowest, believe me, Dryden."

"But she managed to get her money away from him, didn't she?"

"No," Quinlan replied with a shake of his head. "Twice the court has upheld Haislip and the will and the only way she'll ever get her inheritance is when he dies. He's told her she can have it a year after she returns to him. But she'd rather die than go back to him."

"How'd she keep the bank going without dough?"

"With the proceeds from the sale of some property that her grandfather had left her many years before, something that her father appears to have forgotten about and didn't include when he left everything in Haislip's keeping, and with the help of a couple of loyal and trustworthy people who worked for the bank, she was able to keep it going."

"I see."

"She's a good businesswoman, Dryden. As a result, she's developed the bank into an even better paying proposition than it was when it was left to her."

Dryden couldn't think of an appropriate comment, so he held his tongue.

"I'll tell you something I've never told anyone else, Dryden," the attorney continued. "If I could handle a gun properly, I'd have put an end to John Haislip a long time ago. Every time I think of the way he used to abuse and mistreat Marie . . ."

He didn't finish. Tight-lipped, he merely shook his head. Suddenly he pushed the bottle across the table and got to his feet and as he started for the door, he said over his shoulder:

"Help yourself."

Dryden needed no coaxing. He poured himself a third drink and gulped it down. Wiping his lips with the back of his hand, he watched Quinlan open the door, poke his head out, and heard him say something to someone. But it was said in such a low voice, he couldn't make it out. But moments later when Quinlan stepped back, closed the door and turned around, he had a long, flat white envelope in his hands. Returning to his chair, he opened the envelope in such a way that Dryden was able to see what it contained, a package of crisp, new bank notes. The lawyer emptied the envelope on the table and with great deliberateness proceeded to count out its contents, ten one hundred dollar bills, and each one crackled with newness as he handled it. Dryden, who had never seen a hundred dollar bill before, stared at the mounting mass of notes with wide eyes.

"One thousand dollars," Quinlan said, making a neat pile of the bills.

"Yeah," Dryden breathed at him. "That's a lot o' dough."

Quinlan lifted his eyes to him.

"How many men do you suppose wind up a life of privation without accumulating any money to speak of?" he wondered aloud.

"O-h, most, I suppose," Dryden replied. "And a thousand dollars, damned few ever manage to put that much together.

Man who works for a living only makes about enough to get by on. So putting some aside, that's out."

"Just as a matter of curiosity, Dryden, what would you do if you had a thousand dollars of your own?"

"That's a question I don't even have to think about for an answer. I can tell you right off."

"Y-es?"

"If I had a thousand bucks of my own, I'd head straight for California."

"Oh?"

"The way I've heard tell about California, it's big, new country and a man coming out there with a decent sized grubstake in his kick can find any number of ways to double and triple his money and keep on doing it."

The lawyer nodded and said:

"I've heard that too, and I haven't any reason to doubt it." Then in a musing tone he went on with: "So that's what you'd do if this money was yours, climb up on your horse and head west and never draw rein till you crossed the Nevada state line into California."

Dryden smiled a little wryly.

"Yeah, that's what I'd do, all right. Only trouble is I'm shy some nine hundred and ninety-three bucks of having a thousand and chances for makin' it don't look too good," he said.

Averting his gaze and focusing it on the evenly stacked up pile of bills, Quinlan said:

"I know how you can earn that much money and be on your way to California minutes after if you're really as anxious to get there as you want me to think you are."

They sat in silence for a long moment after that.

"John Haislip lives alone about three hours' ride from here," the lawyer said quietly but without looking up. "There's no one within miles of his place so there'd be no chance of interference and no one to point an accusing finger and say . . ."

"That I killed him? That's what you want me to do for you, isn't it, and why you brought me in here in the first place and why you flashed that bankroll on me to tempt me?"

Quinlan lifted his eyes to meet Dryden's.

"Yes," he answered bluntly.

"I kinda figured you had something in mind right off only I couldn't tell what it was till you told me about the girl and that Haislip maverick."

"To make sure that everything goes off without a hitch," Quinlan said, "I'll go with you and point out his place to you. Then I'll back off and wait for you close by. I'll have the money in my pocket and when the job's done, you'll get your thousand and you'll go your way and I'll go mine. We'll probably never see each other again. But we'll know that each of us has done something worthwhile for the other. I'll be helping you get to California, a goal you might never attain by yourself or on your own. In return you'll be doing something for me, indirectly that is, but more directly for Marie. And whatever she wants, I want for her. What do you say, Dryden? Is it a deal?"

There was no need for Howie Dryden to ponder the proposition offered him. Admittedly, at any other time the mere hint of a suggestion that he should kill someone would have frightened him into taking to instant flight. This time though it did not have the usual panicking effect upon him. Perhaps the liquor was responsible for the change that had come over him. Perhaps and very likely it was something else that influenced him. Perhaps he was practical enough to realize that he might never have another opportunity like the one offered him. More than likely though his willingness to consider the proposition was due to his feeling of assurance that he could complete the mission successfully and get away safely. First, Quinlan, the instigator and as guilty as he would be of killing Haislip, had too much at stake to gamble away his future and his life unless he was completely confident that they could get to Haislip without any difficulty, kill him and get away without fear of being even remotely suspected of participation in the crime. Then too Dryden felt secure in his belief that Quinlan would not dare betray him as the killer because he would be putting a rope around his own neck.

"Yeah," he said, trying to make himself sound casual, as though killings were an every day occurrence with him. "It's a deal."

The lawyer nodded and filled Dryden's glass and then his own. As he pushed the silver stopper down into the mouth of the whiskey bottle, he said:

"I'll be ready to ride when you are."

"S'matter with now?"

"I'm ready."

They touched glasses, downed the contents and put down their glasses on the table. Quinlan returned the bank notes to the envelope, folded it in two and put it in his inside coat pocket. He looked at Dryden.

"Let's go," the latter said.

Together they stood up. Dryden stepped around Quinlan to the sofa, picked up his hat and clapped it on his head. Mechanically he curled the brim with his big, awkward hands.

"It might be advisable for us not to be seen together," the lawyer told him. "That is, in town."

"Uh-huh. Think it'd be better for us to meet somewhere's away from here?"

"Yes. A couple of miles north of here there's a sizable cluster of white-faced boulders and rocks. You can't miss the spot. That would be a good meeting place."

"All right with me," Dryden responded. "How soon?"

"O-h, suppose we say in an hour?"

"Right. Want me to go out first, kinda take my time getting up on my horse and so on to make it look good, like I'm not going anywhere special or in a hurry?"

Quinlan nodded again and said:

"When you finally head out of town, go downstreet to the corner and take the stage road west. But after a mile or so, swing north."

"Uh-huh."

"When I'm ready to go," Quinlan continued, "I'll ride in the opposite direction. That is, upstreet and east, then I'll turn north too."

NINE

Sam Priddy, the testy lawman who had told Marie Norton what he thought of her and of the people of Kittings, and who had concluded his embittered denunciation by quitting his job, was not one to lose any time shaking the dust of the town he wanted no more of off his boots. Emerging from his office in full, purposeful stride with his blanket roll slung over his left shoulder, his stuffed-out saddlebags draped over his left arm and his rifle clutched in his right hand, he turned upstreet and headed for the stable two doors down from the far corner. Passersby who greeted him with a word or a nod received a stony, lip-curled stare in acknowledgment. He looked up mechanically when he heard the plod of approaching hoofs. Recognizing the oncoming horseman, he slanted across the walk to the curb and waited there till Dryden neared him. Then he beckoned with his rifle, and Dryden, recognizing him too, pulled up in front of him and leveled a questioning look at him.

"How'd you make out with her?" Priddy asked.

For one fleeting moment Dryden was tempted to feign innocence and counter with: "Huh? Who d'you mean?" But sensing by Priddy's question that the lawman must have seen him entering the bank with Marie Norton and Richard Quinlan, he hastily abandoned the idea and answered with a half-smile and a shake of his head: "They're quite a pair, aren't they, that Marie and that lawyer of hers?"

"Yeah, they're some pair, all right. Only Marie's the worst of the two. When I saw you going into the bank with them I wondered if you were gonna let them sweet-talk you into buyin' what they had to offer."

"I wasn't buyin'," Dryden lied.

"That's good. Quinlan isn't really a bad sort. It's just that he's so blamed crazy about her, he blinds himself to her

68

. . . her rottenness and she takes advantage of it and used him to do her dirty work. He thinks she's gonna marry him some day. I'll bet you anything you wanna put up that she doesn't. If she was of a mind to marry him, she'd have done it a long time ago. She coulda got herself unhitched from the one she's tied to, feller named Haislip, any time she wanted. But she didn't. By keeping herself tied to Haislip, she's able to keep stallin' Quinlan off. Married to one, she can't marry the other. Right? But what gets me is how can a smart, nice-looking feller like Quinlan let her make such a damned fool out've him?"

"Like you said before, Sheriff, he's in love with her, and from what I've heard tell, love is supposed to be blind."

"Yeah," Priddy admitted. "Guess it must be. Oh, was any thing said about Len Shattuck? Either one of th'm mention him, Marie maybe?"

"Uh-huh. Marie. Only I don't remember exactly what it was she said."

"Bet it wasn't anything compliment'ry."

"No, it wasn't."

"She didn't say why she had it in for him though, did she?" Priddy pressed Dryden.

"Nope."

"Then I'll tell you. They tried to talk Shattuck into taking on some kind o' job for them and he turned them down cold. He only told me that much. But not what they tried to proposition him to do. But he didn't have to tell me. There are some things I can figure out for myself, and that was one of them."

"Yeah?"

"I think they wanted him to go after Haislip and gun him down. Fact is, I'd be willing to bet that that was what they wanted him to do. But Len was no hired gun. That's why he turned them down."

Dryden didn't answer.

"I'm glad you didn't let them sweet-talk you into doing the job for them. Which way you heading?"

"West."

"I'm heading south. To Texas. That's where I hail from. I've been away nine years come December and now that I'm my own man again I kinda think I'd like to go home. Sorry you aren't going my way, partner. We'd've been company for each other."

"That would've been nice," Dryden agreed. "Going it alone when you've got a far piece to ride isn't the way I like to travel. But that's the way it happens sometimes. And when it does and there isn't anything you c'n do about it, you quit fussin' and fretting and you make the best of it and hope it won't be that way the next time."

"Only way to look at it," Priddy said.

Dryden had slacked a bit in the saddle, his normally sloping shoulders rounded and hollowed. Now, though, he squared back, lifting his shoulders unnaturally. When he had settled himself and prepared to wheel away, his shoulders sagged and resumed their natural slope.

"We-ll, so long, Sheriff," he said. "Have a nice trip."

"Thanks," Priddy answered. "Same to you."

Dryden gave him a half-salute and backed his horse away from the curb. As he rode down the street, unhurriedly as before, Sam Priddy followed him briefly with his eyes. If he had wondered before about Howie Dryden, wondered what kind of a man he really was, he didn't wonder about him any longer. He knew he would never see Dryden again. With a heave of his body, he turned and went on his way.

For the first time since he had agreed to kill John Haislip, Dryden began to experience some doubts and misgivings. If he hadn't run into the sheriff, he wouldn't have had any reason to wonder if he had done the right thing by himself in making the deal with Richard Quinlan. In an effort to reassure himself he insisted that it didn't matter at all to him that Shattuck had probably been offered the same deal and that he had turned it down. Shattuck was a homeless, footloose drifter who gave nothing and who wanted nothing out of life. He refused to take root anywhere and had no desire to do anything for himself. That, Dryden argued, was where they differed, and the difference between them and the way they looked at life was so important, it served to appease Dryden's conscience. He had agreed to kill a man for pay because he knew it would provide him with what he needed to make something of himself. If he failed to take advantage of the opportunity offered him, in all likelihood there would never be another opportunity to equal it, and he would have no one else to blame for it save himself. There would be others who would gladly snatch up what he had been offered, for life in this uncivilized and violent new land was cheap. Every day men took other men's lives and for far less reason than Dryden's. By the time he had reached the corner, Dryden had convinced himself that he was doing the right thing by himself. He pulled up abruptly when a team-drawn farm wagon came rumbling up, with a man and a bonneted woman riding on the driver's seat and a bawling calf occupying the walled-in body of the wagon, watched it turn and take the stage road west. Then he loped after it.

Converging upon the white-faced boulders that marked their meeting place, and drumming toward it from opposite directions, Dryden and Quinlan spotted each other from some distance off and waved to each other. Minutes later they came together, dust boiling up around their horses' hoofs.

"Have any trouble finding this place?" Quinlan asked.

"Nope."

"When I came out of the bank and happened to glance downstreet I saw you talking with Sam Priddy."

"Sam who? O-h, y'mean the sheriff?"

"Yes."

"He didn't tell me his name. So for a minute there I didn't know who you meant."

"What did Sam have to say?"

"Mostly that he was going back home. Comes from Texas, y'know."

"Anything else?"

"O-h, a little o' this and a little o' that. But nothing much of anything. Y'see, we'd only met for the first time about an hour ago. So being strangers to each other, there wasn't anything much he could have said to me or that I could have told him."

"I see."

"I've been wondering about something. Marie and you seemed relieved when you heard Len Shattuck was dead. Why? He do something to either or both of you that got you two down on him?"

71

Quinlan hesitated for a moment, obviously debating something with himself. But then, apparently having come to a decision, he said:

"I don't see why you shouldn't know. Will it matter any to you if I tell you that Shattuck was the first one offered the . . . the deal?"

"Nope. And you people got sore at him for turning you down. Right?"

"Let me put it this way, Dryden. For a man with his kind of reputation, Shattuck was so contradictory he not only surprised me, he actually amazed me. There was a man who was known to have left a trail of blood and death from the Mexican border to the Canadian, and from Kansas to California. Yet he . . ."

"What it all came down to was that you wouldn't believe he wasn't a hired gun," Dryden said, interrupting him.

"I told you, with his reputation for killing . . ."

"You probably thought he was tryin' to hold you up for more money."

"That's right," the attorney acknowledged. "I was so sure that that was his game, I did something I rarely ever do. I got sarcastic with him and when he stalked out on me, I expected him to square things with me by getting word to Haislip of what I had sought to get him to do. Apparently, though, I misjudged him on that count too."

"Or you woulda heard from the law. Y'got the money on you?"

"Yes, of course."

"My hands are itchin' for it. So suppose we get going?"

"I'm ready."

"Then let's go."

Guiding their horses around the boulders, they rode northward. The terrain was rough and uneven, grassy, thinly though, in some spots but barren and hard-packed in the main. Then it became humpbacked with alternating rises and downgrades. But it finally leveled off only to turn hilly after a couple of miles. There was no conversation for both men were occupied with their thoughts. The only sounds that were heard were the creak of saddle leather and the occasional metallic clatter of ironshod hoofs when their horses pranced over stretches of stony or shale-carpeted ground. The miles fell away behind them. An hour passed, then two. The horses had already begun to wheeze and pant. When they began to labor, their riders slowed them down to a mere walk. Twice the men pulled up and dismounted and delayed their progress in order to give the animals a chance to blow themselves. Each time they stood headbowed and spread-legged with their sweat-coated bodies heaving. But each time after a fairly brief respite they went on again. But at Dryden's instance they made no attempt to urge the horses to go faster. Instead they permitted them to set their own pace. Once, looking around him, obviously for recognizable signs, Quinlan said:

"We're getting nearer."

Dryden's reply took the form of a grunt.

Then a while later, Quinlan called:

"We're nearly there."

This time Dryden didn't bother to answer.

When they came to a trail that wound its way up an incline, Quinlan reined in and Dryden, following the lawyer's lead, pulled up too.

"Yeah?" he asked, easing himself a bit in the saddle. He lifted his gaze up the trail. "Y'mean this is it?"

Quinlan nodded and said:

"When you top the trail, you'll find that the ground falls away in a gentle, grassy slope that leads down into a tiny, saucer-like valley. Haislip's house is right in the middle of it, at the foot of the slope, probably no more than thirty or forty feet from the top of the trail."

"This the only way to get to his place?"

"No. There's a road on the other side, the front of the house. This is the back of it."

"Oh! Kinda thought there had to be a better way than this," Dryden remarked. "And y'say he lives here alone, right smack in the middle of nowhere, with no neighbors or anything?"

Quinlan smiled and answered:

"There's no accounting for some people, for their likes or dislikes, you know."

"We-ll, what does he do with himself? How's he keep himself busy? Man has to do something, or he . . ."

"He has a lot of books and he reads a great deal. It

73

may be that he writes too. That might account for his desire for quiet and privacy. However, that's pure conjecture
on my part."

"Pure what?"

The lawyer smiled again and said:

"Guesswork. I haven't any actual knowledge whether he
writes or he doesn't."

"And this is where Marie lived with him?"

"That's right. And the monotony and the loneliness nearly
drove her crazy. That was one of the reasons why she
simply had to get away from him."

"What am I supposed to do?" Dryden asked. "Ride
straight down to the house, call him out and blast him?"

"N-o, I don't think so. He'll probably hear you coming
and come outside of his own accord. The moment he steps
out, do your job quickly and thoroughly, turn around and
come back up here and we'll conclude our business and
part company."

Quinlan backed his horse out of the way and Dryden
knee-nudged his mount into movement, and with the lawyer's eyes holding on him, started up the trail. But a couple
of feet short of the top Dryden halted his horse and raising
up a bit in the stirrups and then just a little higher peered
over the edge and down into Haislip's valley. Quinlan, eyeing him, frowned.

"Go on, man," he called impatiently. "Go on."

His frown deepened when he saw Dryden swing down
from his horse, suddenly twist around and beckon and
flatten out in the dirt on his stomach and inch his way up
the trail to within touching distance of the top. The attorney, his frown dissolving into a puzzled look, hastily dismounted and scrambled up the trail and knelt down at
Dryden's side.

"What is it?" he wanted to know. "What's the matter?"

"Somebody's standing in the doorway," Dryden told him.
"Get down real low and crawl up a mite past me and take
a good look and lemme know if it's Haislip."

"Oh!" Quinlan said. Disregarding the fact that he was
wearing dark clothes, he obeyed, got down on his hands and
knees and crawled higher up the trail, raised up cautiously
when he reached the top, peered down and quickly worked

74

his way down to where Dryden was waiting. "That's him! That's Haislip," he whispered excitedly. "And he's standing right where you can't miss. Go ahead now and earn your money. Kill him!"

TEN

Slowly propping himself up on his knees and then hastily bending low in an effort to avoid exposing himself to the gaze of the man who was standing in the open doorway of his house, Dryden managed to get the gun out of his holster. His movements were awkward, his big, bony-fingered hands clammy and trembling. The awaited moment for action had arrived but his nerve and his resolve had already begun to falter. He struggled desperately to fight off panic. The thousand dollars that would be his for killing John Haislip was the biggest prize that had ever been offered him, and he wanted it more than he had ever before wanted anything. His one chance of completing his mission and of obtaining the money lay in defying his fears, in shooting before panic overwhelmed him. Richard Quinlan who had backed past him down the trail hissed at him:

"Hurry, man. Hurry, or you'll lose your opportunity."

Dryden wanted to answer. He tried but failed because his mouth, his lips and his throat had suddenly dried up on him. He tried to swallow. But the absence of saliva made swallowing impossible. Struggling frantically now to do the job at hand, he flattened out on his stomach and digging his boot toes into the ground to give him leverage, he pushed and clawed his way up the trail as stones, pebbles and loose bits of dug out dirt rolled down behind him. Wheezing and gasping for breath through his open mouth he reached the very top and looked down. The man whom Quinlan had identified as John Haislip had sauntered outside and was standing half-turned and looking in a westward direction. Raising up again on his knees, Dryden tried to level his gun at his unsuspecting target.

"Well?" Quinlan demanded. "What are you waiting for?"

Dryden's right hand shook so violently, he grabbed the

wrist with his left hand in an effort to steady his gun. There was movement below him, then immediately behind him, and in another moment Quinlan had crawled up next to him.

"What's the matter?" he demanded in an impatient whisper.

"Dunno," Dryden rasped back at him. "My hand's shakin' so and I can't stop it."

The lawyer looked hard at him.

"Don't tell me you've lost your nerve?"

"I . . . I dunno. But all uva sudden I'm shakin' all over," Dryden answered.

He knew what was wrong with him, knew full well that despite his efforts to withstand the panicky feeling that was gripping him, he would have to yield to it. Now his right hand was shaking even more violently than it had before. Cold sweat beaded his face and the clamminess that had been confined to his gun hand now seemed to have spread all over him.

Quinlan was staring at him. Suddenly, and with a muttered curse, the lawyer got up on his knees, reached over and tore the gun out of Dryden's hand. Haislip had turned to re-enter the house. The door toward which he was sauntering was half open. Obviously refusing to be denied that for which he had hired Dryden and determined to put an end to the man who he believed stood in his way, Quinlan stood up, pointed the gun at Haislip and fired. The roar shattered the silence. The bullet went wide of its mark. It struck and splintered the door and flung it back. As it caromed off the wall that right-angled it, Haislip leaped for it, caught it before it could close and was across the threshold in a flash and safely inside the house before Quinlan could get off a second shot. It came just as the door slammed behind Haislip. The bullet struck the ground a couple of feet short of the door and spewed dirt about in several directions.

Allowing his disappointment and his pent up rage at Haislip to goad him to recklessness, Quinlan went skittering down the grassy incline. He yelled something and pegged another shot at his now hidden quarry. The bullet dug its way into the woodwork that framed the door and gouged out a couple of splinters. But then the door opened and John Haislip, holding a half raised shotgun in his hands, stepped out. Quinlan was within a dozen feet of the bottom of the downgrade with level ground immediately ahead of him and Haislip waiting for him. The two men fired at the same time. But the shotgun's blast was louder and more authoritative than the Colt's voice. At practically pointblank range, despite Quinlan's admitted inexperience in handling a gun, there was little likelihood that either man could have missed hitting the other. The roar of gunfire held in the air for a moment. Then it began to lift and presently dissolved. Deep, oppressive silence returned and draped itself over the area.

The stillness helped restore Dryden's composure. Slowly and cautiously too because he had no way of knowing what he would find he raised his head and peered down at the house. He sucked in his breath instinctively and stared with wide eyes. Squarely in front of it lay a man, John Haislip, flat on his back with his legs spread apart and his arms outflung. His shotgun lay in the trampled dirt beside him. Then Dryden spotted Quinlan. He lay face downward in the thin grass at the bottom of the incline with his left arm bent under him and his right arm framed around his head. Shattuck's gun was still clutched in his right hand.

Deciding that he had better get away from there before someone, attracted by the sound of gunfire, appeared and spied him and involved him in what had happened there, Dryden was about to bolt and run. That he had lost the only opportunity he might ever have of getting his hands on some real money came to him as he turned and started down the trail to his waiting horse. Then the thought came to him that he could still have the money, that all he had to do was go down the slope to where Quinlan lay and take it. He turned a second time, retraced his steps up the trail, topped it and made his way down the grassy slope to Quinlan's side and bent over him. Just as he was about to thrust his hand inside the lawyer's coat, he stopped, and frowning, reconsidered. Marie Norton, he reasoned, must have been the one who had furnished Quinlan with the money just as she must have known what it was to be used for, that it was to go to Dryden for killing her husband. If he removed the envelope containing the money from Quinlan's person, when the lawyer's body was discovered and Marie learned that nothing of value had been found upon him, she would know at once that Dryden had taken it.

As he pictured it to himself, she would claim that she had given the thousand dollars to Quinlan whom everyone knew represented her for the purpose of completing a business deal for her. Then she would suddenly recall that Dryden had been present when the money had been handed over to Quinlan. Having thus made Dryden a prime suspect, unwittingly of course, she would continue to remember even more damaging matters. She would recall for instance that she had heard Dryden ask Quinlan which way he was going and that the lawyer had told him. She would say that she hadn't thought anything of it at the time because Dryden had left first and that she had seen him ride downstreet while Quinlan went up the street. Of course once Dryden had left town, she would add, there was nothing to prevent him from circling back and overtaking the lawyer and robbing him and . . . she would stop abruptly and claim she had suddenly realized that she was practically accusing a stranger of robbery and perhaps worse when she really hadn't any reason to suspect him of any wrong doing. Grimly Dryden abandoned the idea of taking the money.

He was glad she couldn't possibly involve him in the double killing. And to clear herself of any connection with them she would admit that Quinlan had often expressed his jealousy of her husband. Reluctantly, perhaps a little tearfully too, she would also admit that on more than one occasion Quinlan had sworn he would kill Haislip. Of course she would hasten to add that she hadn't taken that seriously because Richard Quinlan was not the kind of man who would hurt anyone, let alone kill someone.

So, Dryden expected, the law would absolve her of any complicity in what had happened, and she would concede, tearfully as before, that even though she found it hard to believe, she must have been mistaken in her judgment of Quinlan. But she would have achieved everything and at no cost to her. Her thousand dollars would be returned to her, her unwanted husband would be disposed of and so would the man who had thought that by doing her bidding he was winning her love. But if Sam Priddy was right in asserting that she had never had any intention of marrying Quinlan, then she would be glad to be rid of him too. Her estate that had been entrusted to Haislip's safe keeping would now revert to her, and ironically too, since she was still Haislip's wife, whatever property and money he had left behind would pass to her.

"Some people have all the luck," Dryden muttered to himself. "That's why most others don't have any at all."

The gun that was still gripped in Quinlan's hand caught his eye. He couldn't afford to leave that behind him. Someone, he was sure, was bound to recall having seen him wearing it, and when the law was informed of it, there could be trouble. Since Marie in her feigned innocence had already made him a prime suspect, the law would do everything it could to further involve him. If he left Shattuck's gun behind him, the law might charge that he had shot Haislip, that afterward, in an effort to cover himself he had put the gun in Quinlan's hand to make it appear that the lawyer had killed Haislip. Reaching over Quinlan's body, Dryden pried apart the dead man's fingers, removed the gun and easing back on his haunches, shoved the gun down in his holster. Suddenly it occurred to him that it would never do for Quinlan to be found without a gun in his hand, and that the gun would have to show that it had been fired but minutes before. When a hasty and almost frenzied search of the lawyer's person failed to turn up a gun that he could substitute for Shattuck's, Dryden nearly panicked. Straightening up, he scampered past the sprawled out body of John Haislip with hardly more than a glance at the dead man, and darted into the house. It was some minutes before he reappeared. But when he did, he had found what he had sought, a six-gun that he had come upon in a bureau drawer in Haislip's bedroom.

Remembering that Quinlan had fired four times, he ran to a small clump of painfully thin and scrawny brush, parted it and pointing the gun at the ground, fired four quick shots into it. Now he was satisfied. He would be leaving the scene of the shootout exactly as it had happened. Whoever discovered the two bodies would find all the evidence there that the two men had shot it out and that they had killed each other. Hurrying back to where Quinlan lay, Dryden dropped Haislip's gun in the grass just beyond the curled fingers of the lawyer's right hand. Stepping back, he stood motionlessly for a moment, suddenly jerked himself around and went scrambling up the incline, practically flung himself across the crest, skidded breathlessly down the trail to his waiting horse, hauled himself up on the animal's back and rode away.

Determined to put as much distance as possible between Kittings, John Haislip's isolated place and himself, Howie Dryden refused to allow his horse or himself any unnecessary respites. So two days' hard riding found him some seventy miles northwestward of Haislip's home and even farther than that from Kittings. In an effort to avoid being seen by anyone, he had kept to the hill trails throughout instead of taking to the stage road far below him. But the hills made for rough, toll exacting progress that was wearing on him and torturous on his laboring horse. When the fagged animal began to falter and stumbled a couple of times, Dryden halted him and climbed down. He was so saddle sore as a result of the long haul, he had to stamp about to get the cramped feeling out of his legs and the blood circulating through them again. Hunching his shoulders and twisting his protesting body this way and that he managed to work some of the stiffness out of himself. His horse stood headbowed, with his sweat-matted sides heaving. Yet a couple of minutes later he looked around at Dryden and whinnied: when the latter sauntered back to him and patted him, the horse whinnied again and nuzzled Dryden's arm and shoulder.

Deciding that he would be courting trouble for himself if he continued to keep to the hills and acknowledging that he had been lucky so far in avoiding a laming or crippling mishap to his horse, Dryden conceded to himself that he had no alternative but to head downgrade to the stage road. The narrow, twisting trails with their stone-and-shale surfacing and upended rocks here and there posed a constant threat to a fresh and alert horse. To a tired horse they were even more of a hazard. Leading his horse, Dryden and the animal threaded their way through rocks and boulders, a necessarily slow and time consuming process that held more than a mere sprinkling of danger. A dozen times the leg weary horse lost his footing on the smooth, stone surfaced-down trails and slid. Fortunately though he managed each time to stop himself from piling into Dryden and crushing him against an unyielding boulder or a rock pile. And half an hour later when they emerged from the hills and stepped on level ground both breathed a deep sigh of relief. Standing on the shoulder of the ribbony span of road, Dryden ranged a look behind him and then ahead of him. But as far as he could see the road was deserted. Snorting and pawing the ground with his hoof, the horse indicated that he was ready to go on. Dryden swung himself up into the saddle and as he settled himself, the horse trotted away with him. Dryden hoped he hadn't broken from cover too soon. Still, he maintained, seventy miles or so was a lot of distance and he felt reasonably secure. Of course if his luck held, and if Haislip's and Quinlan's bodies weren't found right away or for another couple of days, it would give him even more time to put even more distance between Kittings and himself. He had made no attempt to urge his horse to quicken his pace, choosing instead to leave that to the horse. Suddenly, though, he was aware that the horse had broken into a lope. He smiled a little, leaned forward and patted the animal.

Suddenly though, so suddenly in fact that Dryden fell forward and had to hang on to save himself from being thrown, the horse broke stride and stopped. Forcing himself up into a normal sitting position, Dryden looked up wonderingly. Then he realized that the horse's unexpected halting was the animal's way of calling his attention to something ahead of them, something that might mean trouble or danger to Dryden. Raising up a bit in the stirrups, Dryden peered hard. A couple of hundred yards ahead was something that suddenly came erect and dissolved into an arm-waving and beckoning woman. Nudging his horse with his knees, Dryden rode on and presently came up to her and leveled a surprised look at her.

ELEVEN

Howie Dryden made no bones about it. He was a poor judge of ages, and he admitted it quite readily. To him people fell into two classifications. Either they were young or they were old. It didn't seem to matter much where men were concerned. They didn't appear to care about their age, gave it quite freely when they were asked, and without any hesitation. Yet he would have been hard pressed to recall when he had last heard a man ask another man how old he was. He couldn't even remember the last time anyone had asked him his age. It was, he had learned a long time before, a different story where women were involved. While he had known but few women in his forty-one years, and none of them very intimately, from those with whom he had come in contact he had learned that women in general resented getting old far more than men did. They took offense and got angry when they were asked how old they were, and when they had no alternative and had to answer, they assumed a defiant and belligerent attitude and invariably lied.

He judged the woman who stood before him at his horse's head to be somewhere between twenty-five and thirty-five. He knew that women aged faster in the west than they did elsewhere. Primitive living conditions took its toll of them. So he was reluctant to do any more than approximate her age. She was rather pretty, but in a hard-eyed and bold way. There was something familiar about her, not about her personally because he knew he had never seen her before. She wore the recognizable stamp of a saloon or gambling casino steerer. She was one of those women whose job it was to get lone men to buy liquor, then it was up to them to induce them to gamble.

He stared down into her face with her hard, shiny eyes lifted to him, her rouged cheeks flanking a rather nicely shaped nose, her rouged lips parted in a smile that revealed a red smear or a smudge on her teeth. She wore large gold earrings with some kind of multi-colored stones in them. But the gold wasn't real; some of it had already begun to tarnish. A frilly ribbony and feathered hat was perched on her head of reddish-brown hair, and a short, unbuttoned jacket that she wore over a blue silk dress that was low cut and showed much of her chest completed her costume. The dress was snug-fitting, actually a little too tight for her. It spanned her hips and moulded her breasts so that they stood out boldly from her chest. Then he glimpsed a cloth-covered valise behind her. When he had first spotted her, she must have been sitting on it, he told himself.

"We-ll?" she asked with an even deeper smile than the one she had flashed at him when he had come up to her. "The way you've looked me over makes me wonder. You've seen a woman before, haven't you?"

He crimsoned and answered:

"Yeah, sure."

"Oh. For a minute there you made me wonder if you were one of those . . . what d'you call them? Hermits? You know, the kind who bury themselves high up in the mountains and never come down out've th'm to see what the rest of the world is like and the people in it. I've been told that some of them have never seen a woman."

Still flush-faced, he said a little lamely:

"Guess finding you alone out here in the middle of nowhere kinda surprised me."

"Wanna know something? Finding myself out here like this surprised me, too. But it's my own fault. Instead of taking the stage like I intended, I let some drummer in a buggy sweet-talk me into letting him drive me. When he forgot that he was supposed to be a gentleman and thought he had me where he wanted me and got fresh with me, I whacked him good. He got square with me by dumping me out."

"Where were you headed?"

"The way you're going," she told him. "I'm going to pay someone a surprise visit."

"Uh-huh."

"I had just about decided that there wasn't any use

waiting any longer for someone to come along and that I'd better start walking. But just at that moment I saw you coming, and I was never so glad to see anyone as I was to see you. Walking is fine for those who like to walk. But not for me. Guess I was built for comfort, and that means riding when I'm going somewhere."

"Whereabouts is this place you're headed for?"

"I don't know exactly 'cept that it's out this way, off this road about a hundred feet in from it. Mister, I'll pay you if you'll give me a lift to where I'm going. How about it? You wouldn't go off leaving a lady sitting out here all by herself, and as you said, in the middle of nowhere, now would you?"

Drydon didn't answer. He simply dismounted. The woman came forward. He helped her poke her foot into the stirrup, helped her climb up into the saddle. She straddled the horse, pulling up her ankle-length dress to free her legs. When she saw him stare at her uncovered legs, she smiled a bit and asked:

"S'matter, Mister? Has it been that long since you last got a look at a woman's legs?"

Embarrassed again and flushing again, he caught up her valise and handed it up to her. She was about to put it in front of her when she stopped and asked:

"You're going to get up here too, aren't you?"

"N-o, don't think I oughta, Ma'm," he said with a shake of his head. "Y'see, I've come a long ways and I've been pushin' my horse real hard. Carryin' the two of us might be just a mite too much for him right now."

"Oh," she said, settling the valise squarely in front of her and holding the handle with both hands. "I don't like putting you out like this."

"Forget it. I don't mind doing a piece of walking. Might take some of the stiffness outta me."

She arched her eyebrows and said:

"All right, if you say so. O-h, what's your name?"

"Dryden, Ma'm," he replied over his shoulder as he reached for the bridle to lead his horse. "Howie Dryden."

"Mine's Serena Fears, and I'm pleased to make your acquaintance, Mr. Dryden."

He murmured an indistinct response.

" 'Course," she went on, "if you were to come into

the place where I work and you asked for me, nobody'd know me. That is, nobody 'cept the boss. You've been in Tiny Oliver's Paradise Cafe, haven't you?"

"N-o, 'fraid not, Ma'm."

"In Quemado," she added, as though she expected that that would refresh his memory.

"Quemado?" he repeated. "Where . . . where's that?"

"Mean you've never heard of it, or of Tiny or the Paradise either?"

"Nope."

"And I thought that just about everybody'd heard of all three. Quemado's right on the border between Texas and Mexico, and the Paradise is supposed to be the biggest cafe anywhere. We-ll, maybe not exactly anywhere. There are a couple of places in Kansas City that might be a little bigger. But I'll bet we get an even bigger play than they do. Anyway, that's where I work, at the Paradise. O-h, and about my name there. Tiny didn't think it was right for his place and his customers. So he made me call myself Pearl."

He thought about it for a moment, then he said:

"I suppose one name's as good as another. But for my dough, Ma'm, and if you don't mind me sayin' so and right out too, I kinda think I like Serena better."

"I do too," she confided.

"Got something to it that Pearl hasn't got. Y'know?"

"I know. But Tiny's the boss."

"Uh-huh, and what the boss says goes."

"That's right."

Dryden led his horse for a time. Then he released his hold on the bridle and let the horse, too tired to do anything more than plod along, go on as he saw fit. He glanced at Dryden, apparently unable to understand why his master was walking while someone else was astride him. He turned his head and gave the Fears woman a long, searching look.

"We-ll, now, isn't he the nosy thing," she said and she laughed, and Dryden, occupied with his own thoughts, jerked around and lifted questioning eyes to her. "Your horse," she told him. "He just gave me the same kind of looking over that you did."

They went on then in comparative silence after that,

with nothing but the thump of the horse's hoofs and the occasional squeak of saddle leather to shatter the silence.

"You aren't married, are you, Mr. Dryden?" Serena asked.

"No, Ma'm," Dryden answered, over his shoulder as before.

"That's what I thought. And what I don't understand is how come a man like you, nice and decent and respectful, hasn't found a woman who has enough sense to know something good when she sees it. I declare, I don't know what women can be thinking of these days. I know there are lots more men out here than women. But most of the men I see aren't the kind a woman would give a second thought to. They're footloose or on the dodge. So a good man is still mighty hard to find." She paused, seemingly to give Dryden a chance to comment. When he didn't take advantage of the opportunity, she went on with: "One of these days you'll meet up with a woman who can see past the end of her nose and who has some good sense in her head and that'll be it for both of you."

A mile gradually slipped away behind them, and then another. Progress was necessarily slow because the plodding horse showed no inclination to quicken his pace and Dryden, trudging along at his side, made no attempt to hurry him. A deep stillness held over the area, and the road ahead of them, practically ruler-straight, was deserted.

"It's a good thing for me you came along, Mr. Dryden," Serena told him, settling herself again after twisting around for a look behind her. "Or I might have had to sit there right through the night and maybe into tomorrow waiting for someone else to come by. And somebody else mightn't've been as nice as you. S-ay, you always so quiet or does it only seem that way to me because I like to talk and probably don't give anyone else a chance to get in a word even sideways?"

This time when Dryden looked around at her, he smiled.

"Got things to think about," he replied, "and I'm the kind that can't think and talk at the same time and do right by either one. So if I'm kinda quiet, like I said, it's because I'm thinking and not because you talk too much and aren't giving me a chance to do some for my-self."

"Oh," she said, apparently satisfied with his answer. "You live around here, Mr. Dryden?"

He shook his head.

"No. Just pushin' on west and hoping to work my way out to California," he told her.

"California, huh? I hear it's real nice out there. You been there before or . . ."

"This'll be the first time for me."

The plodding, hoof-thumping horse suddenly broke into a jog and Dryden had to lengthen his stride to keep up with him. As a precaution in case the unpredictable animal decided to run and outdistance him, Dryden grabbed the bridle and held on to it securely.

"What happened to him so all of a sudden-like?" Serena wanted to know, clinging to the pommel with one hand and to her valise with the other.

"Dunno," Dryden flung back at her over his shoulder. " 'Less he suddenly got tired of just crawlin' along."

They went on for a time after that without any further conversation. The jogging horse soon resumed his uneven plodding, Dryden released his hold on the bridle and Serena sat back more comfortably again. Dryden, lifting his gaze skyward, announced without turning to Serena:

"Clouding up."

"Oh, no!" she said unhappily. "Don't tell me its going to rain. If it does, I'll be a mess when we get there."

"Gettin' darker."

"Oh, why couldn't it have waited till later!"

Dryden had no ready answer for her, so he held his tongue.

It began to drizzle, gently and with a feathery touch. Frowning, Dryden halted his horse, unstrapped his blanket roll and digging inside of it, found and hauled out his poncho, strapped up the blanket and moved to Serena's side.

"Gimme the bag," he said to her. He didn't wait for her to hand it to him; he simply took it from her. "Now take off your hat and put it in your lap."

She obeyed, quickly unpinned and removed her frilly headpiece and moved it into her lap and held it there with one hand. With the other hand and with Dryden's help she managed to get the poncho over her. Reaching up, he drew it up a bit from behind her so that it covered her head too. He hung the valise from the pommel, stepped back from her and whipped up the collar of his shirt around his neck and buttoned it. He yanked down the brim of his hat to shield his eyes from the thickening drizzle, took hold of the bridle and jerking it, led the horse on again. The rain began to pour down. The horse snorted protestingly. But when Dryden paid no attention to him, he subsided and tramped on headbowed.

"You all right, Serena?" Dryden asked, raising his voice against the drumming rain.

"Yes!" she answered in a muffled voice. "But you must be drenched!"

"Some," he acknowledged. "But this isn't the first time I've got soaked and chances are it won't be the last. So don't worry yourself none about me. I'll make out all right."

The rain pelted down upon them, turning the road into a sea of mud and water. It obscured Dryden's vision too despite his anxious efforts to peer through it in hopes of spotting a shelter of some kind. There was a sudden, awesome crash of thunder, and a stab of red and yellow light, a startling flash of lightning, that blazed through the sky, burning a fiery path through it and then was gone. But it served a worthwhile purpose. It lasted but a moment, but just long enough to reveal to Dryden the presence of a low, stubby structure some distance inland from the road.

"Think I've found us a place!" Dryden yelled to Serena. "Hang on now!"

He led the horse off the road and into some grass at the side of it, and practically dragged him up an embankment that confronted them. Topping it and stepping onto level ground, Dryden forced the wornout horse to jog, and running at the animal's side, guided him toward what he had already decided was a line rider's shack. As they neared it, Dryden, peering through the swirling, and now windblown rain, thought he saw a faint glow of lamplight sift out through the shack's window. It enabled him to see that it wasn't a line rider's shack, but a fairly good sized cabin with twin windows flanking the door. As they panted up to the cabin, Dryden yelled. The door was suddenly opened and a man with a half-raised rifle in his hands filled the doorway, silhouetted by lamplight that flickered behind him.

TWELVE

"Yeah?" the man asked, peering out at Dryden, then lifting his eyes to the hunched-over figure sitting astride the latter's horse, and then returning his gaze to Dryden. "Who are you, and what d'you want here?"

Before Dryden could answer, Serena cried:

"Augie, it's me, Serena!"

She flung herself off the horse with an abandon that startled Dryden as well as the horse, and raising her dress, presenting a distorted and unflattering view of herself with the shapeless poncho bulging out in front of her due to her hat that she was holding under it and against her body, and scampered up to the man in the open doorway. He stared at her.

"What . . . what are you doing here, Serena?" he demanded of her, but without moving aside to permit her to pass.

She laughed, a little wildly Dryden thought as he looked on.

"What kind of a way is that for a man to greet his wife?" she retorted with something of a chiding, saucy touch to her tone. "And get out of the way, you big ox, so I can come in out've the wet."

The man named Augie shrugged.

"You c'n come in if you want to," he said, lowering his rifle. "But you're wrong about being my wife, Serena. You haven't been for some time now."

She squeezed past him, turned and called:

"Come in, Mr. Dryden, and meet my husband. All of a sudden he seems to've found himself what he must think is some kind of a sense of humor."

Augie backed inside, holding the door wide for Dryden who halted in the doorway, took off his hat and half-turning, shook off some rainwater that had accumulated on it, and stepped inside. The warmth of the softly lighted cabin reached out and embraced him.

"Ah," he said to Augie with an appreciative smile. "Sure feels good in here."

Augie didn't answer. He closed the door and backed against it. He was a big man, as tall as the lanky Dryden, and brawny. His broad shoulders spanned the door behind him. He propped up his rifle against a chair that stood nearby.

"I met Mr. Dryden on the road," Serena told him, bunching up the poncho in front of her, reaching up under it and removing her hat, and letting the glistening poncho drop again. She put the hat on a table just beyond her. "Got any hot coffee, Augie? I could go some. And I'm sure Mr. Dryden could too. He made me wear his poncho. Even with that on I got me a chill clear through. And he must be soaked right through to his skin. Y'know, if it hadn't been for him, I'd have drowned out there." She looked down at the table. Her eyebrows arched. A clean and freshly ironed red checkered cloth covered the table, and on top of the cloth and squarely in the middle of it was a small but gracefully shaped bowl with a lacy doily under it. "For a man who never cared whether there was a cloth on the table, you've changed, Augie, and for the good. And the floor looks like it gets swept every day and washed too. Guess I'd better leave you alone more often. Looks like leavin' you on your own is what you've needed."

There was a light step, a flowered floor-length curtain opposite her was whisked aside and a slim, pretty girl appeared. Serena eyed her and frowned.

"Looks like I've been giving you too much credit, Augie," she said. "How long has this been going on?" Dryden sensed that there was going to be trouble and wished he had declined Serena's invitation to come inside and that he had gone on his way. She took a step toward the girl. "All right, you. Get your things and clear out before I throw you out. Go on now."

"Don't pay her any mind, Ellie," Augie said, and came away from the door to the girl's side and curled a muscular arm protectively around her waist. "If you'd listen once in a while, Serena, instead of always runnin' off at the mouth, you might get to hear something. I told you before you aren't my wife and haven't been for some time now. Fact is, more'n eight months now. But you thought that was funny, didn't you? But it isn't so funny now, is it?"

She stared at him with wide eyes and with her mouth open a bit too.

"I told you, Serena, that if you went off and took that job workin' in a saloon that you didn't have to come back because I wouldn't be there. But you went anyway, didn't you, not carin' a whit whether I liked it or not. We-ll, long's that was the way you felt about it, I went to see ol' Judge Ames and I told him we were through and that I wanted things done legal-like. He fixed up some kind o' paper for me to sign, and when I'd put my name to it, he said that was it. I was free of you and you were free of me. Divorced, he called it. Couple o' months after that I met Ellie and married her. I'm right happy with her too, and I think she is with me. What's more, she's doing something for me that you wouldn't do. She's carryin' my baby."

Dryden had been shuttling his gaze between the two, focusing it on Augie when he was speaking and then shifting it to Serena to see the effect on her of Augie's words. Now his eyes held on her. He saw her swallow hard, saw her lips come together and tighten into a thin, red line, saw her jaw muscles twitch and her hard eyes burn.

"Now there's no point in you makin' a to-do about this, Serena," Dryden heard Augie continue quietly and evenly. "What's done is done and there isn't anything you c'n do to undo it. So rain or no, I think you'd better get yourself together and get out of here. You too, Mr. Dryden." Dryden felt his cheeks flush. "I'm not holdin' anything against you because there isn't anything to hold against you. But Ellie's a kinda delicate girl and being that she's in a family way, excitement of any kind is bad for her. So we want to be left alone nice and quiet-like because that's the kind we are."

He gave the girl's arm a little squeeze, gave her a re-assuring smile too, and walked to the door and waited there with his hand on the knob. Serena looked hard at Ellie, then turned her back on her.

"All right, Augie," she said. "I'm going. But you haven't seen or heard the last of me. I'm not finished with you or with her either," and she jerked her head in the girl's direction. "Come on, Mr. Dryden. Let's get out've here."

"Right," Dryden said and he put on his hat.

Serena joined him. Suddenly though, before he realized what she was up to, and before he could do anything to prevent it, she had yanked the gun out of his holster, whirled and leveled it at Ellie. The terrified girl screamed. There was a deafening, thunderous roar of gunfire that rocked the cabin and made the little bowl on the table jump. Dryden winced and blinked. Serena gasped and tottered, turned on buckling legs and sagged headbowed against Dryden who raised his arms around her instinctively. A great sob broke from her. Slowly she slipped through his arms and crumpled up on the floor at his feet, eased over on her back with her arms outflung and with his gun still in her hand. Dryden stared at her, turned his head and looked doorward at Augie. But Angie wasn't there. Dryden turned the other way and saw Augie kneeling over his wife who lay outstretched on the floor.

"It's all right, honey," he heard Augie say to her. Then the big, brawny man came erect with her in his muscular arms.

Dryden saw him brush aside the curtain with his arm and carry Ellie into the next room, obviously their bedroom. As the curtain dropped gently in place behind them, Dryden moved with a sudden swiftness that belied his usual hesitancy and awkwardness. Telling himself that he had to get out of there in a hurry if he wanted to avoid becoming involved in something that was not of his doing and that might easily lead to trouble for him, he bent over Serena, snatched the gun out of her numbing hand, holstered it and straightening up at the same time, headed for the door. As he reached it, he stepped on something, stopped and looked down. It was a rifle. He remembered having seen Augie prop it up against a nearby chair. Moving alertly though when he saw Serena grab his, Dryden's, gun, and level it at Ellie, he must have caught up his rifle and fired instantly. And when he had seen his wife topple he must have dropped the rifle in his frenzied haste to get to her. Dryden kicked it away, sent it slithering away over the floor. He opened the door and bolted out.

The rain hadn't let up any. It was still pelting down. His

horse stood headbowed and dejected looking, with water dripping from him and the rain drumming on the surface of the saddle. Dryden ran to him, hoisted himself up astride him, wheeled him and despite his nasally voiced protests, lashed him and sent him bounding away toward the road. Just in time, and just as they neared the embankment, Dryden remembered it, and pulled the panting horse to a skidding stop, and let him make his own way down to the road. In another moment or two, they were loping westwardly over the road that was as thoroughly deserted as it had been earlier.

It had already occurred to Dryden that by fleeing he was depriving Augie of the only witness to what he would claim in his own behalf, that he had shot Serena in his wife's defense. Admittedly it would go hard with him if the law refused to believe his story or his wife's. Grasping at straws, at anything that might ease his conscience, for it was already beginning to trouble him, Dryden took refuge in what he had long heard said, even though he didn't fully believe it, that truth would out, and somehow, he insisted to himself, it would in Augie's case and he would be freed. If he had stayed to help Augie clear himself, he was afraid that the law might probe a little too deep into his own most recent activities, and that he might find that in helping Augie he had made trouble for himself. He was sorry for Augie. But he had to think first of himself. It was a selfish attitude to take. But self-preservation made it necessary.

The rain, he suddenly noticed, had begun to slacken off. He was suddenly aware too that his horse had slowed his pace of his own accord and was jogging. The rain continued to abate and finally stopped altogether. A ground haze rose up and for a time trying to see about him was like trying to see through a gauzy curtain. But when he happened to look up, he spotted an expanding patch of blue in the sky. He watched it widen and when it finally filled the sky, the haze dissolved. The air was still damp, but it smelled clean, as though it had been thoroughly washed, the grass richly green though raindrop beaded and giving off a sweet, flower-like fragrance. He was hungry and uncomfortable because his wet clothes clung to him. He reached behind him and touched his rolled up blanket. It was thoroughly soaked. When he happened to look south-ward and spied some ranch buildings a mile or so away, he pulled up so abruptly, it brought a snort of protest from his horse. A moment later though he nudged the animal into movement, wheeled him off the road and headed for the place he had just spotted. He hadn't intended stopping any-where as long as his horse could keep going for he was anx-ious to get as far away from Augie Fears' homestead as he could. But he wasn't equal to his resolve. He had to have something to eat and a chance to dry himself out before he could go any further.

Apparently the horse must have understood why he had been guided off the road, that is, once he caught sight of the place toward which they were headed. He seemed to sense the nearness of hay and oats and a dry, com-fortable stall in which to rest himself, and eager to get to them, summoned what little strength he had left in him and broke into a fast trot. As they neared the ranch, a barn loomed up on the left. Opposite it was a low, squat build-ing that Dryden quickly recognized as a bunkhouse. Be-yond it and diagonally opposite the barn was a corral, its gate open and hanging a little crookedly, and its smooth-worn bars wet and glistening. Some fifty or sixty feet farther on was a sprawling ranchhouse with a veranda en-circling it. There was no one about, no sound of anyone either. As he came closer to the barn his practiced eye took note, critical note too, that it was badly in need of repair, and he shook his head. Ranching was a business just as storekeeping was and the man who permitted his property to run down usually found that his business was deteriorat-ing too. As he approached the barn, he slowed his panting and laboring horse to a walk; when he came abreast of it, he pulled up and peered inside through the wide-open doors. But it was gloomily dark in there and he couldn't see anything. He shifted his gaze to the bunkhouse. The door to it was ajar and the small windows that flanked the door were empty, paneless frames and looked as though someone had gouged the glass out of them. A musty air of abandon-ment drifted out of the bunkhouse and made Dryden screw up his face and wonder if anyone lived on the place or if the owner had simply given up on it and gone off.

He walked his horse up to the house, dismounted and hitching up his levis climbed the three steps to the veranda, crossed it to the front door and raised his hand to knock. He felt eyes on him and he stayed his hand and turned his head. In the thin shadows cast off by the house, a woman in dark, drab clothes who was sitting motionlessly on an up-ended wooden box about a dozen feet away met his eyes. Across her knees was a rifle.

"Oh," he said, touching his hat to her. "Didn't see you sitting there, Ma'm, till just now."

"What do you want?" she asked in a dull, toneless voice.

"Got caught in that rainstorm and got myself soaked clear through," he told her. "On top o' that, I'm so blamed hungry, I . . ."

"Inside," she said, interrupting him. "You'll find some cold meat on the table. There's a pot of coffee on the stove. Put a light under it."

"Why, thanks, Ma'm," he said. "I'm sure obliged to you."

There was no response. He opened the door and went inside. Fifteen minutes later when he came out again, the woman was still perched on the box and in the same spot.

"Feel like a new man," he told her, closing the door behind him.

"You'd better get those wet clothes off," she said. "Go down to the barn. You'll find some work clothes hanging on a hook. Take what you want of them. My husband won't be needing them any more. So you might as well have them."

"Yes, Ma'm," he said.

Obviously her husband had died and probably hadn't been dead very long. That accounted for the dark clothes she was wearing and for her dull, listless tone and manner, and indicated that the shock of his death hadn't yet worn off. He wondered if he shouldn't have said something more, perhaps offered a word of condolence and sympathy. He would do that later, he decided, before he was ready to go. He clapped on his hat and turned to go down the stairs.

"Don't step on him," she said and he stopped instantly and looked back at her. "He's laying where he fell. Just inside the doorway."

Dryden stared at her and at the rifle too and wondered

97

if she had been the one who had cut down her husband. He had heard of such things before. Starvation and privation could do strange things to people, and that included husbands and wives. It could make people hate each other and could lead eventually to . . .

"I tried to move him," he heard her say in her flat, lifeless voice. "But I couldn't. He was too big and too heavy for me. So I had to leave him there." Dryden held his tongue because he thought it wise and because he couldn't think of the right thing to say. "O-h, if only he had listened to me. But he didn't, and now he's dead."

Then she hadn't done the shooting. Someone else had. Dryden was relieved.

"You . . . you know who did it?"

"Yes," she answered simply.

"Oh?"

"It was his partner, Gene Costa. Steve hadn't liked him very much at the beginning. But he was sure he could handle Costa and keep him in line. Unfortunately when Steve found he couldn't, he didn't have the money to buy Costa out. And he was unwilling to clear out and leave everything to Costa. I was willing, though, even though it meant losing everything we'd put into the place, and I tried to talk Steve into agreeing. But he wouldn't. Somehow Costa had got the idea that since they were partners that he was to share me with Steve. Instead of working the place, they did nothing but hang around. Costa with a smirk on that evil face of his and a look in his eyes that I didn't like, and Steve unwilling to leave me alone with Costa around."

"H'm," Dryden said, shaking his head. "Heckuva setup, all right."

She ignored Dryden's comment and continued with:

"Things finally came to a head at noon today. They had words, exchanged a couple of punches and wound up shooting it out. It would have been better if it had been Costa and I who had shot it out. Steve was handier with his fists than he was with a gun. I can handle a gun with any man."

"This Costa feller, he got away, huh?"

"Yes. But I don't think he went very far. I think he's holed up somewhere close by and that he'll be back. For me. He'll probably wait till it's good and dark so he can

98

slip up on me undetected. I'll be waiting for him. But not with open arms as I'm sure he hopes, now that Steve's out of the way. I'll be waiting right here, in the darkness and with this rifle, and I'll kill him, the rotten swine.

THIRTEEN

They talked a bit more after that. Actually though it was the woman who identified herself as Dora Welling who did most of the talking and Dryden who save for a minute comment here or there who did most of the listening.

"I've been keeping you standing here talking when I should have told you to go right down to the barn and get out of those wet things and into some dry ones," she said.

"It's all right, Ma'm."

"No, it isn't," she retorted severely. "Go on now."

"Yes, Ma'm," Dryden said dutifully.

"Then I think you'd better get up on your horse and go on your way. I don't want you hanging around here and getting yourself mixed up in something that doesn't concern you."

As he trudged down to the barn, his water-logged boots squeaking and squishing in the wet grass and in the muddied, puddled dirt, he couldn't help but wonder why he seemed to be fated to go from one piece of trouble to another.

"Damned if I c'n understand it," he complained bitterly to himself. "I don't go looking for trouble. Fact is, I shy away from it. But doggoned if it isn't there waiting for me the minute I come along. Gettin' so, I'm beginning to think I'd better give people a wide berth and keep to myself, because people mean trouble."

His frown had already become a full-fledged scowl.

"Now take that business with that gally young squirt Clete Ainslee," he continued. "There I was right after I'd hit that lousy town, alone at the bar in Andy Horvath's place, drinkin' a beer and aimin' to head out again right after I was finished. But Mister Ainslee and his crusty idea walked in on me and right off I was in a bind same's everybody else in the town. Then the next town I hit I had to get myself mixed up with Marie Norton and that Quinlan feller. I was damned lucky to get myself outta that mess. But right off I bumped into Serena and there I was again in another mess, this time with a man, the woman who used to be his wife and the one who took her place. Good thing for me I didn't lose any time getting myself the hell away from them, or I mighta been in for something."

He paused and shook his head.

"So what happens? I stop by here lookin' for some grub and a chance to dry myself out and what do I find starin' me right in the eye? More trouble. A woman with a gun waiting to gun down the man who gunned down her husband. Oh, I'm running in luck, all right. Only it's all bad. Now it's got me wondering what else is waiting to happen to me, and if there's ever gonna be an end to it."

He had no answer for himself, no way of assuring himself that it wouldn't always be like that, that bad luck usually ran just so far and so long, that after a while, after it had run its course, it would fade away and that good fortune would replace it. He came up to the barn, halted in the open doorway and poked his head inside the shadowy and musty smelling structure. A little beyond the doorway and sprawled out on the dusty floor on the flat of his back was the body of a man, a big, burly, barrel-chested man. There were scrape marks on the floor that began at the door and ranged back from it, thin, uneven tracks that had been made by his bootheels when he had been dragged back from the doorway and out of sight and gun range of the man who had shot him down. That was why Dryden hadn't been able to see him laying there when he had reined in at the door and peered inside. Treading carefully to avoid stepping on the dead Steve Welling's hands, Dryden moved inside the barn, stopped when he was clear of the dead body and looked down.

"Poor devil," he said half aloud.

Then he wondered what the Welling woman intended to do about her dead husband. She couldn't leave him laying there indefinitely. She would have to have him buried. Deciding that it wouldn't be wise of him to ask her for fear that she might ask him to dig a grave and while he was about it do whatever else might be necessary to prepare the body for burial. Dryden looked about him for the old clothes that had been offered him. He found them hanging from a wall hook. Just past it and diagonally opposite the doorway were two stalls, one of which was occupied. The horse that was the occupant whinnied when he became aware of Dryden's presence and nearness. He whinnied eagerly, almost pleadingly. When Dryden ignored him, he pawed the floor a couple of times with his hoof and slapped the stall wall with his tail in an effort to attract Dryden's attention. The latter leveled a look at him, sauntered over to the stall, patted the animal on the rump and told him:

"It's all right, boy. Everything's all right. So take it easy."

The horse shrilled happily as Dryden patted him once or twice more. But Dryden had to move alertly and side-step to avoid being trampled as the horse, apparently expecting to be led out of the barn and away from the dead man, began to back out of his stall. When Dryden stopped him, he snorted protestingly; when Dryden turned away from him, he whinnied pleadingly. But Dryden disregarded him. He was more interested in the dry clothes that had been offered him. He found them hanging from a hook in the barn wall. Just as he was about to lift the first thing, a pair of levis, off the hook, the muzzle of a gun was jammed hard against his spine. He froze instantly with his right hand in midair.

"That's it, partner," a man's voice said behind him. He winced inwardly when the muzzle dug even deeper into him. "Hold it just like that." He felt his gun being lifted out of his holster. Then the pressure of his captor's gun was eased. "All right. You can turn around now," he was told. "But do it careful-like and not too sudden. I've got a nervous trigger finger and when my hand jerks, my finger does too and my gun goes off. So watch it."

Slowly Dryden turned around. The man he found facing him was lean and a little taller than average, his face thin and dark, his eyes hard and shiny. Dryden took it for granted that the man was Gene Costa. If he was, then it confirmed Dora Welling's belief that he hadn't gone very far off.

"What's this all about?" Dryden asked. "What . . .

102

what's the idea of jumpin' me like this? I haven't done anything."

The muzzle of Costa's gun pressed lightly against Dryden's flat belly.

"I'll ask the questions," Costa answered curtly. "All you have to do is answer 'em." Dryden grunted. "Who are you and what are you doing here?"

Simply and without any embellishment Dryden told him.

"That's all she told you?" Costa pressed Dryden. "Just to help yourself to whatever you wanted of the stuff you found hanging in here?"

"That's right."

Costa gave him a hard, disbelieving look.

"Mean to tell me she didn't say anything about him?" he demanded with a jerk of his head in the direction of the dead man.

"Just that I'd find a dead man layin' in here and for me to kinda watch my step."

Costa's lips curled a bit.

"Didn't you think it kinda funny for her to tell you he was dead and then not tell you any more like what'd happened to him?"

"Mister," Dryden replied, "I learned a long, long time ago that the best I could get outta askin' questions about things that didn't concern me was trouble. So what I don't get told I don't ask. Besides, I don't know him," he went on with a glance at Steve Welling. "So while I'm sorry for him same's I would be for anybody else in the . . . the fix he's in, soon's I get outta these wet clothes and into some dry ones, I aim to do like she told me to."

"Yeah?"

"I'll get up on my horse and go on my way."

Costa's gaze held on Dryden for another moment. Then with his own gun still pressed into the latter's mid-section, he hefted the Shattuck gun, glanced at it, murmured something of a surprised 'H'm', brought it up a bit higher so that he could get a closer and better look at it, and said:

"Pretty fancy gun you're wearing. Where'd you get it?"

"Offa somebody who didn't have any more use for it."

"What's that supposed to mean?"

"You ever hear of Len Shattuck?"

Costa's eyes came up again to meet Dryden's.

"Len Shattuck?" he repeated. "You mean Len Shattuck the gun fighter?"

"Uh-huh."

" 'Course I've heard of him!"

"That was his gun. I got it offa him."

Costa frowned and demanded:

"What do you mean, you got it offa him? A gun fighter's gun is his . . . his whole stock in trade. Without it he's lost because no other gun ever feels right to him. Yet you want me to believe that Shattuck gave you his gun just like that."

"I didn't say that."

"Damned good thing you didn't," Costa retorted, "because I wouldn't've believed you. What'd you do, steal it from him when he was asleep?"

"Nope. I took it offa him after I killed him."

Costa stared hard at Dryden. His frown deepened and darkened his face even more than it was normally.

"You killed Len Shattuck?"

"Uh-huh."

"I don't believe you," Costa said flatly.

Dryden's shoulders, rounded and sloping ordinarily, lifted together in a ruler-straight shrug and promptly slumped again.

"That's all right," he said simply. "You can believe whatever you like. Only you oughtn't ask a man a question when you know aforehand that you don't aim to believe his answer."

Gene Costa refused to let Dryden's mild criticism of him force him to retract or even temper his outspoken disbelief.

"You don't look like a gun fighter to me," he insisted. "Or like a man who'd dare take on a gun fighter."

"I've been told that before."

"And I'll tell you something else that I'll bet you've been told before too," Costa continued, and this time rather heatedly. "I think you're exactly what you look like. A saddle tramp."

"Like I said before, Mister, you can think anything you like. All right if I take those things," and Dryden jerked his head at the dry clothes hanging just behind him, "and get outta here?"

"Yes, take th'm and clear out!"

Half-turning, Dryden reached up, lifted the pieces of clothing off the hook and draped them over his left arm. Then squaring around again he held out his right hand mutely to Costa.

"Yeah?"

"My gun," Dryden said, still holding out his hand for it.

"You can't have it," Costa answered him. "I don't think it's yours to begin with. I still think you stole it from Shattuck. On top o' that there's something about you that I don't like. I don't know exactly what it is, so I can't put my finger on it. But it's there, all right. So because of that I don't feel that I can trust you. I don't think I oughta take a chance letting you have a gun on you. You got what you wanted here, didn't you, some grub and some dry clothes? Then get out've here."

"That gun belongs to me," Dryden protested. "So you haven't any right keepin' it."

Holstering his own gun and shifting the Shattuck gun to his right hand, Costa leveled it at Dryden.

"Get out've here, I said!"

"All right, Mister," Dryden said with another lift of his shoulders. "If that's the way you want it. Only for your sake I hope nothing happens to make you sorry about this." Circling around Costa who turned with him warily, Dryden started for the door, carefully stepped over Welling's body, and halting in the open doorway, looked back at Costa and said: "Just came to me that I left my horse standing in front of the house."

"O-h, you did, huh? Then you hold it right there," Costa commanded. Still holding the gun on Dryden, he came forward. "If you think I'm gonna let you go up to the house and tell Dora that I'm holed up in here, you've got another think coming. Back in here, you. That's it. Now suppose you turn yourself around and go find yourself a nice quiet little spot in one of the empty stalls and stay put there till I say it's all right for you to come out? Go on now," Costa ordered him, gesturing with the gun.

Dryden did not protest. Passing the horse in the only stall that was occupied, ignoring the animal's low-voiced whinny, he stopped when he came abreast of the very last stall in the four stall row. He draped the dry clothes over the stall wall. Actually the wall was only a thin-boarded and flimsy partition that stood about four feet high and served to separate the stalls from one another. Thumbing his water-logged hat up from his forehead, he took it off and laid it on top of the heaped up clothing. Backing out of the stall, he ranged his gaze doorward in search of Gene Costa.

"Hey," he called when he spotted the man standing motionlessly in the thin shadows a couple of steps back from the open doorway and looking toward the house. "All right if I shuck these wet duds and climb into the dry ones?"

"I don't give a damn what you do," was Costa's curt and disinterested reply.

"Nice friendly feller, all right," Dryden murmured to himself.

Minutes later when the change had been completed and the wet pieces of clothing had been spread out to dry over the stall wall, Dryden glanced doorward again. He had heard something heavy being moved a few moments before. Now he saw what it was, a heavy, wooden chest that Costa had dragged out and on which he had perched himself on just about the same spot on which he had been standing. Apparently he wasn't overly concerned about Dryden's jumping him for he had shoved Shattuck's gun down inside the waistband of his pants. Eyeing him, Dryden wondered what the Welling woman would do if she knew how really close by Costa was. Dryden wondered too what would happen when darkness set in and if as Dora Welling expected Costa would slip out of the barn and try to get into the house without being detected. He couldn't understand why Costa hadn't fled for his life. Unless of course he intended to stand his ground and claim that he had slain Steve Welling in self-defense.

"I kinda think he'll have a helluva time gettin' the court to go for that," Dryden told himself. " 'Less he can get the Welling woman to testify for him. But in view of what she told me, that she aims to kill him, I don't see how that can happen."

Apparently though Costa refused to believe that Dora Welling didn't like him.

"Must be he thinks she does, but that she couldn't let

106

on because of her husband. But now that he's dead and outta the way, Costa must think she wants him to make her give in to him but that she wants him to make the first move so it'll look like it was all his doing and none o' hers. Maybe he thinks that that way it'll be easier on her conscience."

From what Dryden had seen of Dora Welling, and he admitted it wasn't very much, she was about as plain and unattractive a woman as he had ever laid eyes on. Yet Costa was not only willing but eager to risk his life in order to possess her.

"Only way I can figure it," Dryden concluded, "is that he must see a helluva lot more in her than I do."

He stopped his conjecturing instantly and looked up when he heard sauntering, crunching bootsteps. Costa, with his thumbs hooked in his belt, stood in the doorway. He was motionless for a moment or two. Then he straightened up, dropped his hands and stepped out of the barn. Curious to see what would happen, Dryden hurried to the doorway and stole a guarded look outside.

FOURTEEN

Dryden was somewhat surprised to find that night had already fallen. Admittedly he shouldn't have been for he knew that in the open range country there was no gradual transition from dusk to night, just the barest and briefest interlude between the two. But while his eyes had become accustomed to the thin shadows that had filled the barn earlier and he had become aware that they had deepened steadily, dimming and then practically obliterating his surroundings, even things within reach but minutes before, he had failed to recognize that as an indication that it was night. A dozen feet from the barn was a back-turned, shadowy figure of a man, Gene Costa, standing motionlessly in the path that led to the house some thirty feet away. One moment it was draped in veiling shadows. Then as Dryden, lifting his eyes to it, watched, it became steeped in gloomy, distorting darkness. Trying to pierce the darkness with his searching gaze, he sought a sign of the Welling woman and wondered if she was still sitting on the veranda with her rifle laid across her knees as he had last seen her. But nothing moved on the veranda and no sound came from it. He wondered if time might have weakened her avowed determination to kill the man Costa, wondered if after her rage had had a chance to spend itself if she had undergone a change of heart. Even assuming that she hadn't, that she was just as determined as before to exact vengeance from Costa, he wondered if she would be strong enough to go through with killing him when the time for it came. It was one thing to vow to kill someone. It was something else again when the moment for it presented itself and demanded that it be acted upon at once or that the revenge seeker back down. It made him a little sick to his stomach when he thought of how close he had come to killing someone. It

108

was all he could do to rid himself of the scene that suddenly came to mind of him raising his gun at John Haislip, and Richard Quinlan, crouching beside him and urging him to shoot.

Despite his wondering about Dora Welling he had the feeling that she would do exactly as she had said she would. So she was probably still sitting on the veranda, as motionless and as silent as the night itself, and waiting patiently for Costa to come to her. Not suspecting what she planned to do to him and unaware that she was laying in wait for him, Costa would have no reason to temper his wanting of her with caution. And once he came close enough to the house, the embittered woman would turn her rifle loose on him and riddle him with a withering blast of gunfire. He would be dead before he struck the ground.

Suddenly Dryden became aware of a third person's presence, of someone who was standing between the barn and the halted and backturned Gene Costa who was still looking at the house and obviously debating something with himself. Guardedly, even though there was nothing for him to fear, Dryden stole a look at the shadowy figure. He promptly caught his breath. It was a woman. He knew it couldn't be anyone but Dora Welling. She was holding something crossed over her body. When a thin, errant ray of light suddenly glinted on it and then just as suddenly dissolved again he knew what it was, a half-raised rifle.

"Stand where you are, Costa," he heard Dora say, and he thought he saw the man stiffen. "I've got you covered. If you move a muscle, I'll put a bullet in you."

"Now take it easy, Dora," Costa answered without turning around. "You don't want to do anything to me any more than I'd want to do anything to you. You know I'm crazy about you and that I have been all along. Ever since the first time I saw you. And I know you like me too. Only you've never let yourself go enough to admit it. Now why don't you give yourself a chance? Put up your rifle and . . ."

"You filthy, murdering swine," she fairly spat at him. "So you're crazy about me, are you? And you think I like you too. The gall of you! I'll tell you how much I like you. I don't think anyone has ever despised anyone else as much as I do you. Now get your hands up!"

"Dora, will you please? . . ."

A rifle cracked suddenly, ominously too. The unexpected burst of gunfire made the unprepared Dryden jerk and flinch.

"You'd better do as I say, Costa," he heard Dora say. "Or next time I'll shoot at you, not over your head."

Dryden's wide-eyed gaze, shuttling between the two people involved in the drama that was being enacted before him, held on Costa. He saw the man's hands come up and slowly climb half-bent above his head.

"You there in the barn," Dora called, and Dryden, hesitating at first, finally stepped outside.

"You . . . you want me, Ma'm?" he asked her.

"Yes," she told him. "There's a lantern hanging from a wall peg just inside the doorway and you'll find some matches on the ledge just below it. Will you light the lantern, please, and bring it out here?"

"Yeah, sure," Dryden replied.

He turned on his heel and trudged back inside. He reappeared a minute later with a brightly burning lantern swinging from his hand. The light flickered and sputtered momentarily when a breath of night air swirled around the lantern. But then it spun away and the light steadied and burned brightly as before.

"Where d'you want me to put this?" he asked.

"Over there," Dora instructed him, pointing with her left hand. "On the ground between us. That's it."

Having put down the lantern as he had been directed to, Dryden began to retreat to the barn. Dora stopped him with:

"There's another lantern in the barn on the floor against the back wall. Will you make a light in that one, too? You'll need it to see to harness the horse for me."

Dryden grunted a throaty and indistinct response. He acknowledged that he owed her something for the food and the dry clothes, and if this was to be the way in which she wanted him to repay her, he was willing to do what she asked of him. He hoped it wouldn't go beyond what she had already wanted done. As he turned to re-enter the barn he wondered what she wanted with the

110

horse. He hadn't seen any sign of a rig or a wagon. However, if she wanted the horse harnessed he would oblige her and what she did with the horse once he had harnessed him and led him out, we-ll, that was up to her. He found the second lantern almost at once, found it by stepping on its metal base a scant moment after he had returned to the barn and started looking for it. When he had made a light in it and put it down in the middle of the hay-strewn floor and took a step toward the first stall, he stopped and looked down at the sprawled out body of Steve Welling. He would have to move the dead man out of the way before he could lead the horse out of the barn. Bending and forcing his hands under Welling's armpits, he dragged the body back from the open doorway. When he came erect again he was wheezing a bit. He backed the horse out of his stall, spied some worn harness hanging rather limply from a nail at the top of the stall partition and lifted it off. Minutes later he led the animal out of the barn. The horse whinnied happily and turning his head nuzzled Dryden's shoulder. The latter patted him a couple of times and told him he was a 'good boy.'

"There's a wagon behind the barn," Dora Welling said. "Will you? . . ."

"Right," Dryden said simply and led the horse around the building to the rear of it.

He returned shortly with the horse hitched to and hauling a light ranch wagon.

"Just a minute, please," the woman said. "You, Costa. With your left hand. Unbuckle your gunbelt and let it fall."

Dryden, standing silently at the horse's head, watched as Gene Costa, with the lantern's eerie yellowish light playing over him, unbuckled his belt and let it drop at his feet.

"Now kick it behind you," Dora instructed him.

Costa obeyed. With a backward thrust of his leg he sent his gunbelt slithering away. It spun to a stop a foot or two short of the lantern.

"Turn around," Dora ordered. When he turned and stood facing her and she spied the butt of his own gun poked out of the waistband of his pants, she frowned and said curtly: "All right, Costa. With your left hand again . . ."

He had jerked out the gun before she could finish. He tossed it in the dirt. It slithered and spun around and finally stopped when it collided with his belt. Dora flashed him a hard look. Then half-turning to Dryden, she said to him: "Will you give him a hand, please," and she indicated Costa with a nod, "getting my husband into the wagon?"

Dryden rubbed his bristly chin with the back of his hand.

"Gonna take a lot o' doing, Ma'm," he replied somewhat doubtfully. "Maybe too much for just the two of us." He looked back into the lantern-lit barn. "Big man, y'know, and heavy."

"Yeah," Costa added. "And dead weight too."

Dora ignored him.

"I think the two of you can manage," she said evenly to Dryden.

"Come on," Costa said gruffly. "What does she care if we tear the guts out've ourselves doing it?"

He came striding forward and with Dryden following him led the way into the barn. When they had dragged the body of the dead man across the barn floor to the very edge of the doorway they found that the Welling woman had maneuvered and backed the wagon up to it and had even dropped the tailgate to make matters a bit easier for them. It took every ounce of their strength to lift the body and dump it quite unceremoniously on the floor of the wagon. Both men were panting and heaving when they stepped back. It was Costa though who raised the tailgate back in place and who secured it.

"Thank you," Dora said to Dryden. "You've more than repaid me and I'm grateful to you for your help. Now I think you'd better get up on your horse and go on your way."

Dryden acknowledged with a nod. Hitching up his belt and tucking in the tail of his shirt, he trudged over to where Costa's gunbelt lay, bent and yanked Shattuck's gun out of the holster and shoved it down in his own holster, and straightening up, started up the path to the house.

He slowed his step and looked back over his shoulder when he heard Dora say:

"All right, Costa. Climb up in the wagon with Steve."

"What . . . what's the idea? What are you aimin' to do, Dora?"

"You'll find out soon enough. Go on. Climb up there."

"You aimin' to take me into town and turn me over to the law?"

"Just do as you're told," Dora answered, and Dryden, yielding to his curiosity, halted and squared around. He saw Dora gesture with her rifle.

"I dunno what to make of you, Dora," Dryden heard Costa say with what was doubtless a puzzled shake of his head. "You've always been on the kind and . . . and we-ll, gentle side. All of a sudden though you've changed. Guess you kept this side of you covered up, huh?"

"Get up there with Steve," she repeated stonily and levelled the rifle at Costa.

"All right, Dora," the latter said with an empty gesture of his hands and a rather helpless lift of his shoulders. "Whatever you say. Only here's something you oughta think about before we go any further. You turn me over to the law and you'll be sorrier than you've ever been in your whole life. I'll tell the court that you put me up to killing Steve, that you got me so blamed crazy with promises of what was gonna be between us once Steve was out of the way that I wasn't responsible for what I did."

She made no response. So Costa continued with:

"Don't you go thinking for even one little minute that the court won't believe me. O-h, the judge'll give me all kinds of hell for being such a weakling and he'll probably call me every name he can think of. But this sort of thing has happened so many times before, and you wanna know how it's wound up most of the time? I'll tell you. With the man getting off with a light sentence and the woman getting it good. Swinging from a rope or rotting away the rest of her life in prison. Now you think that over, Dora, and you tell me if you still wanna go through with this."

"I had no intention of turning you over to the law," Dora said, and Dryden, unwilling to miss hearing the rest

113

of what she was going to say, found himself retracing his steps down the path to within ten or perhaps fifteen feet of where she was standing. "There wouldn't be any point to it because you've been tried already, and according to law no one can be tried twice for the same crime. Now for the last time, Costa, get up in the wagon."

The rifle came up and held on a line with his chest. He eyed it, looked hard at her, and muttering something under his breath, started to climb up into the wagon. But he stopped suddenly, and lifting his gaze past Dora to Dryden, called to him:

"Hey, you, whatever your name is! I dunno what she's up to but I don't think it's anything good. So don't just stand there. Do something. Stop her from doing whatever it is she's fixin' to do. Y'hear?"

"Don't go mixin' me up in this," Dryden said and began to shy away, backing again up the path.

"Climb up, Costa," Dora told him.

Costa hauled himself up into the wagon and straddling the dead body of Steve Welling, stood facing Dora.

"I'm up," he said gruffly.

"As I said, you've already been tried," Dora said evenly. "By me. And you've been found guilty. Now all that remains to be done is for sentence to be pronounced and carried out."

"Now, wait a minute, Dora. You can't . . ."

As though she hadn't heard him, she said:

"Gene Costa, I find you guilty of murder in the first degree, and I hereby sentence you to death."

"For God's sake, Dora, will you listen to me for just one minute?" Costa pleaded with her.

The rifle roared and Costa gasped when the slug slammed into him, doubling him over. He had just about forced himself up when Dora shot him a second time and then a third. Swaying drunkenly and tottering on buckling legs, he put out his hands, obviously seeking something to cling to. But there was nothing. His open handed arms dropped and hung limply at his sides and his head bowed. He sagged, and crumpling up, slumped down brokenly in the wagon across the body of the man whom he had slain earlier.

As the wide-eyed, in fact bulgy-eyed, and open

mouthed Dryden looked on, Dora lowered her rifle, crossed the few intervening feet of space to the side of the wagon and peered over it at Costa. When she nudged him with the rifle and he failed to move, she stepped back. Shifting the rifle to her left hand, she used her right hand to pull herself up to the driver's seat. Settling herself in it, she propped up the rifle next to her, picked up the reins, looked at Dryden who was still staring at her, and said with such complete calm that it rendered him speechless:

"In case you're wondering where I'm taking them, I'm heading for town. I want Steve to be buried properly. He was a good man and he deserves the best I can give him. Then I'll turn Costa over to the law. I didn't want any part of him when he was alive and I don't want any part of him now that he's dead. So I'll leave it to the law to do with him as it sees fit. And if the law should decide to hold me for killing him, I won't mind. Nothing matters any more. So I'll be right there, and no one will have to come looking for me. Bye."

"Bye," Dryden responded, finding his voice much to his surprise.

He wanted to add 'Good luck'. But she had already driven away, gone before he could voice the words. Turning after her, he ranged his eyes after the jouncing, rumbling wagon till it had disappeared into the night and the blanketing darkness. He tramped up the path to his idling, headbowed horse, hauled himself up into the saddle, wheeled the animal around and started off in a westerly direction. What he had witnessed had shaken him, had left him feeling limp just as all other scenes of violence had effected him. He had to get away from there, quickly too. When he jerked the reins, a signal to his horse to quicken his pace, the animal snorted protestingly. But Dryden was in no mood for consideration or compromise. While he acknowledged that it was one thing to cater to and bow to the wishes and demands of other people, conceding that that was something that he had been doing almost all of his life because he had had no alternative, it was something else again to bow to the whims of a horse. He rebelled and quite openly and firmly. He whacked the horse with his open hand, a stinging, explosive slap on the rump that so startled the unwilling

animal that he bounded away as though he had been catapulted through space and galloped furiously as though he
could feel the devil himself breathing down the back of
his neck.

FIFTEEN

A shoddy, thin-worn blanket that was still rainsoaked offered Howie Dryden but little protection against a stiffening wind that swept over the open range and blew steadily colder as the long night wore on. To add to his discomfort, the wind, swirling about with a startlingly human-voiced drone, spun topsoil about and flung it over him. Then with a show of further contempt for him, it caught up dead, curled up leaves and tiny, broken bits of twigs and showered him with them. Since he had already discovered that he had neglected to transfer his handful of matches from the wet, patched levis that he had discarded in exchange for Steve Welling's dry work pants, a fire was an impossibility. Laying back on the thinly grassed ground with his saddle serving as a pillow, a hard and unyielding one though, and with his hat covering his face, he tried to sleep. He was tired enough. But aside from a couple of isolated brief naps, sleep continued to elude him. With his long arms wrapped tightly around his shivering body and his bony knees drawn up and nudging his belly, he sought doggedly to induce sleep. When his efforts proved futile, he gave up and lay there huddled up, listening to the drone of the wind and to the other night sounds, and to the ground pawing and snorts of complaints of his horse, indications that he disliked the inconsiderate behavior of the elements as much as Dryden did. Finally at dawn, probably because he was exhausted by then, Dryden dozed off and fell into a sound sleep. He awoke with a start and a phlegm-throated cry of protest when a booted foot collided with his ribs. Opening his sleep-laden eyes and twisting around, he found himself staring up into the beady-eyed and unshaven face of a man who was holding a gun on him, Shattuck's, he quickly discovered when he touched his holster and found it empty.

117

"All right, you," the man began curtly. "Who are you and what are you doing out here?"

"Name's Dryden and I'm cuttin' across country to California."

The man grinned evilly, his whipped back lips revealing short, stubby teeth that were black at the gumline and yellowish at the chipped tops.

"Hope you make it," he said dryly. "But don't count on it. Come on," and he gestured with the gun. "Up on your feet."

"What . . . what's the idea?" Dryden asked, struggling up into a sitting position.

"What's doing in town? How many posses they got out now looking for me?"

Dryden shook his head.

"I wouldn't know," he replied. His hat had slipped off his face while he had slept and lay next to him on the ground. As his captor watched, he caught it up, clapped it on his head and quite mechanically curled the brim with his hands. "Y'see, I haven't been in or even near a town for days."

"You on the dodge too?"

"Heck, no," Dryden said quickly.

"S'matter, you broke?"

This time it was Dryden who grinned, a little sheepishly though.

"Just about," he admitted.

"Thought so, or you'da put up at a hotel instead of bedding down out here in the cold. And if you don't mind me sayin' so, Mac, you're a kinda mangy lookin' critter. O-h, not that I look any better. If I look the way I feel, I must be pretty scurvy looking." The man rubbed his unshaven chin with his left thumb. "I think you'd better trail along with me, partner. For a couple o' days anyway. I'll feel safer that way. No point leaving you out here for the law to find and get you to talk and tell them that I'm still around. Better to let them think I've hightailed it. Then after maybe another day of chasin' their tails around looking for me and not finding any sign of me, they'll call it off. Then I'll be free to get going on my own and taking my own sweet time about it. What'd you say your name is?"

118

"Dryden."

"Mine's Clarkin. Toby Clarkin. Up on your feet, Dryden. Time we were getting away from here."

Obeying, Dryden climbed to his feet, grimacing though because his body was cold-stiffened and achy from the hard-packed ground.

"Look, Clarkin," he began. "One thing nobody's ever been able to say about me is that I run off at the mouth. Now if you'll lemme be instead o' makin' me trail along with you, if a posse catches up with me and starts firin' questions at me, I won't know what they're talking about. How about it?"

"Saddle up," was the curt answer and Dryden shrugged and turned away.

"Damn the luck," Dryden thought to himself. "That's all I needed, meeting up with him. Wonder why the law's after him?"

Clarkin's horse was idling close by; when he whistled, the horse shrilled an immediate response and came trotting up to him, nuzzled him, whinnying the while, and was patted in return. Then Clarkin swung up astride him, and settling himself in the saddle, called impatiently to Dryden:

"Come on, man. What's taking you so long?"

Dryden looked around at him.

"My hands are cold and I'm all thumbs," he replied.

Clarkin frowned, but he made no comment. He sat his horse quietly and watched as Dryden, muttering to himself, finally managed to complete saddling his horse, strapped on his wet blanket, and with a plainly painful effort hoisted himself up on his horse's back. With the beady-eyed man leading the way and half-turning around every little while to look back at Dryden and for a quick scanning of the slowly awakening range behind them, they headed southwestwardly. The dew-wet grass that carpeted the range glistened as the early morning sun flooded the sky with bright light and promptly began to burn off the chill that had carried over from the previous night. When Clarkin twisted around and beckoned, Dryden rode up alongside of him and lifted questioning eyes to him.

"When'd you eat last?" Clarkin asked.

His own holstered gun, Dryden noticed, rode on his hip

while the stone-studded butt of Shattuck's gun jutted out of his belt. Dryden had already noted the presence of a rifle in the hunted man's saddleboot.

"Last I ate was late yesterday afternoon," he said. "Woman gave me some cold meat. She gave me these clothes too."

Clarkin grinned at him.

"Kinda wondered if they were really yours," he said, "or if there was supposed to be somebody else in them with you. Mite big for you, aren't they?"

"Her husband was a big man."

Clarkin held his tongue.

"Where are we headed for?" Dryden asked him.

"My camp," he was told. "Got me a nice, snug hole-up in the hills. When we get there, I'll fix you something that'll chase the cold out've you good."

"Uh-huh. All right if I ask you something else?"

"Like why the law's after me?"

"Yeah."

"My partner, Link Wriggins, and me decided that that sleepy little jerk-water town looked like easy pickings. So bright and early yesterday morning we jumped the feller who was opening the bank and made off with the strongbox. Link who was always just a little too quick for his own good and sometimes for mine too to shoot first and ask questions afterward cut down a couple o' characters who happened to come along just as we broke out've the place. They didn't look like much to me, not like the kind who'd have the guts to try and stop us. But they must've looked like the trouble kind to Link, or maybe he wasn't taking any chances with them. Whatever it was, he blasted them good. We got away all right even though some folks pot-shot us."

"Where's he now, this Link feller, waiting for you back at camp?"

Clarkin's face took on a grim look.

"He's dead," he said rather gruffly, and his jaw muscles twitched a couple of times.

"Oh," Dryden said. "How . . . how'd it happen?"

"When we were loopin' it hell-bent-for-election for the hills," Clarkin related, his face still grim but his tone milder, "his horse stepped in a gopher hole and threw him.

120

When I was able to pull up and ride back and got down to have a look at him he was dead. He'd broken his neck."

"Helluva thing to have happen," Dryden commented.

"You can say that again. His horse was all right though 'cept that he couldn't run. Being that he was able to walk, I boosted Link up on him and lashed him on. It was a damned good thing for me that the folks back in that half-baked hole-in-the-wall town hadn't got together yet and come after us. If they had, they'd have got me for sure because we weren't making any time by then. Just about crawling along. But luck was still with me. We made it up into the hills. I cut Link down, dug him a grave, wrapped him up in his blanket and buried him."

"Nobody c'n ever say you didn't do the right thing by him," Dryden said.

"Wasn't any more than he woulda done for me."

This time Dryden made no attempt to answer.

"We grew up together, Link and me," Clarkin continued. "In Oklahoma it was. We hit it off right away. We got to be closer than brothers. Fact is, a lotta folks thought we were. We went through a helluva lot together. But we always managed to get outta trouble with a whole skin. But now he's gone, and I'm feeling it already. I'm alone with nobody to turn to. When a man gets used to running in double harness, makin' him run single stinks."

They drummed on over the sun-swept range in silence after that, Clarkin still grim-faced and bitterly silent, and Dryden unwilling to intrude upon him and his thoughts.

"I suppose I shoulda stayed put up in the hills," Clarkin said finally, and Dryden half-turned his head to him. "But I was kinda curious to see what was doing. So I rode down for a quick look-around. There wasn't any sign of a posse. Guess they must've headed for home once it got dark last night and it began to blow up. And once they got home they musta decided to stay put for the night. A warm, comfortable bed beats the hell out've sleepin' out even when you've got the best blanket money can buy. I figure they'll be hitting the saddle some time this morning, but not till after they've had their breakfast. This posse business is a laugh, y'know that, Dryden? Damned little ever comes of it 'cept that those who've been deputized wind up with stiff backs, cramped legs and sore backsides from riding around in circles like a bunch of jack rabbits chasin' their own tails."

Again there was silence. But it didn't last very long, hardly more than a moment or two. Again it was the man Clarkin who shattered it. He laughed suddenly, a strange, wild sort of a laugh that startled Dryden and made him eye his captor wonderingly and with some misgivings.

"Didn't tell you what I found in that strongbox when I shot off the lock, did I?" Clarkin asked. When Dryden shook his head, Clarkin went on with anger tingeing his voice: "The bastids, they sure made suckers out've us. We shoulda suspected something when we saw how easy they'd made things for us, keeping that lousy strongbox right out in the open where everybody could see it and suckers like Link and me would grab it thinking we were makin' a real haul for ourselves. 'Course there wasn't any dough in it. Nothing but bags of sand."

"I'll be damned!"

"You and me both," Clarkin said angrily, and added in a bitter voice: "That's what Link died for. A lousy box of sand."

"And the two he cut down in town," Dryden reminded him gently. "That makes three of th'm who died for nothing. Helluva price to pay for a box full o' sand."

"Yeah," Clarkin said heavily. "But I wasn't thinking of those other two. They don't mean anything to me. But Link did. Y'know what woulda happened if he'da been alive and he'da seen what was in that box? He'da been so mad at those people for suckering us, we'da gone back to that town that same night and we woulda shot up the place. O-h, woulda fixed those people good. But he had to go and get himself killed."

Lifting his gaze, Dryden could see low lying hills southwestwardly with taller, towering and more rugged hills rising up behind them.

"That's gonna be home for us for the next couple of days," Clarkin said with a nod at the hills. "Y'know something, Dryden? From just about any spot up in those hills, a man with a rifle, enough ammunition and enough grub to keep himself going can hold off a small-sized army. That's why a posse will only go so far after somebody who gets the jump on them and beats them to the hills. If they ever tried to flush anybody outta there, they know he could cut down every last one of them tryin' to reach him. So once we hit my camp, we'll settle down and stay put there, and soon's I figure the law's quit looking for me, we'll break out and get going."

"Uh-huh," Dryden said thoughtfully, wondering the while if Clarkin would really let him go.

"So you're heading for California," Clarkin said in a musing tone.

"That's right. And if I'm lucky, I'll make it."

Dryden was disappointed when his words failed to draw any assurance from Clarkin. It made him wonder and worry even more than before.

"You been out there before?" Clarkin asked him, turning his full gaze upon him.

"Nope. Be the first time for me."

"Got anybody there that you're itchin' to see?"

"Nope," Dryden said again, shaking his head. "Wanna get out there because I've heard tell that it's big, new, beautiful country, and rich country, too. That's for me because the way I see it, a man should be able to do a helluva lot more for himself in a place where there's dough than he can here."

"Right," Clarkin said, nodding, and told him: "I got the California bug myself some time ago and I tried to talk Link into pulling outta here and heading west. But he wouldn't go for it. He argued that the grass always looks greener in the other feller's yard than it does in your own, and kept insisting that one place is as good as another if you hit it right, and that sooner or later we'd hit it good right here. So knowing Link, I didn't mention it again because I knew his answer would be the same as it was before. He was that kind. Once he made up his mind to something, that was it, and nothing and nobody could ever change it. But thinking about you heading there, and listening to you talk about it, I'm hot for it all over again."

"Nothing to stop you now from going there."

"I know. And this is what I've decided to do. We're gonna be together for a couple of days. If we hit it off together, and I don't see why we shouldn't, once we're able to high-tail it away from here, we'll head for California together." Dryden gulped and swallowed hard. "But we'll have to have some dough in our kick. I haven't got a helluva lot, a couple o' bucks at the most, and I don't think you can have any more than that or even that much."

"Got so little," Dryden said with a thin smile, "I don't even bother to count it. I'm afraid that if I do, I'll find I've got even less than I thought."

Clarkin grinned at him.

"Then don't count it," he said. But then he was serious again. "On the way we'll keep our eyes peeled for a small town that looks like there's dough in it. And when we hit one, and it figures we oughta because there must be a lot o' th'm between here and California, y'know, off the . . . the beaten path and tucked away in out've the way places, that'll be it for us. We'll play it smart and cozy so's not to get anybody suspicious, stay over for a day or two to look around and kinda get the feel of things. Once we know where the dough is, we'll make our move, go after the dough, grab it and hightail it. How's that sound to you, Dryden? All right?"

Dryden knew he had no alternative if he wanted to stay alive but to agree to anything and everything that Clarkin might suggest. He would steal a leaf from Clarkin's book and 'play it smart and cozy' himself. It wouldn't do for him to make the man doubt him. Of course it would be a far different story when the time came for him to take a hand in whatever it was that Clarkin had decided they would do. He would find a way, he assured himself, of avoiding active participation in it. But for the time being . . .

"Yeah, sure," he replied. "Sounds fine to me."

His unshaven and beady-eyed companion who had played the role of captor up to a minute before but who was now making him his partner in crime, nodded and went on with a crooked little smile:

"I'll promise you this much, Dryden. Nobody'll sucker us the way Link and me let ourselves get suckered. We won't go knockin' ourselves out luggin' away any strongboxes. If there is one, we'll bust the thing open right then and there and help ourselves to what's inside of it. And it'd better be dough or somebody'll get it good for tryin' to play fast and loose with us. Y'know, you only have to get suckered once to wise up to things. That is, less you're dumber'n all get-out. And we're anything but. Right, partner?"

"Right."

"O-h, this gun of yours, Dryden," Clarkin said, hefting it and eyeing it admiringly. "It's a beaut, all right. I've kinda taken a shine to it and if it's all right with you, I'd like to keep it. I'll give you mine for it and I'll throw in another promise to kinda, we-ll, not only sweeten the swap for you but even it up. I'll make this up to you one way or another. All right?"

As before, Dryden had no alternative but to agree.

"Yeah, sure, Clarkin," he said. "A gun's a gun no matter how much you fancy it up. Sure, you can keep it, and if you don't make it up to me, I still won't complain."

"You're all right, Dryden," Clarkin told him, "and I'm damned glad I met up with you. But just because you're the kind you are, I'll make sure I make it up to you. Here," he said and he jerked out his own gun and passed it to Dryden, who nodded and shoved it down in his holster. Then Clarkin holstered the other gun.

SIXTEEN

The off-the-beaten-path town of Starbuck had come into being many years before as a link in a steadily expanding chain of wayside stagecoach stations. With the passing of time and the swelling westward surge of new opportunity seeking Americans it was to be expected that here and there some California-bound people who had wearied of the long haul should decide that they had gone far enough and chose to settle close by the station. More and more people joined them and the settlement built around the station mushroomed into a town that took the name of the man who had founded and operated the station. Northward there was a handful of fair-sized ranches. But on the other three sides there was nothing save the open range. Once upon a time great herds of buffalo had roamed the rolling plains. Indians of many tribes had hunted the plains and there were still some traces of their villages. But the buffalo had gone and since the Indians had been dependent upon them for meat for their own use and for their hides for trading purposes, they had been forced to strike their tepees and move on in search of other and still virgin hunting grounds.

Starbuck had progressed, but only up to a point. That was when its progress had stopped, and apparently it had stopped for good. Far removed from the usual wagon train routes and more or less isolated, there was little chance of anyone's happening upon Starbuck save by accident. Despite the fact that the originally laid out street that comprised the town had twice undergone lengthening at both ends in order to accommodate new arrivals, the town, now drab to the point of shabbiness, seemed to have resigned itself to eventual oblivion. No new businesses or new families had moved into Starbuck in more than a dozen years. What should have given the town heads even more food for thought and worry was the alarming rate at which the old citizens were dying off, creating a void that showed no sign of being filled. Questionably, some of them must have thought about it and very likely talked about it too. But from all indications nothing was done about it.

Since strangers had become a rarity in Starbuck, it was only natural that the law represented by Sheriff Neil Haley and his deputy, Gil Watrous, eyeing two newcomers with more than ordinary interest from behind the half-curtained window in the sheriff's office, should wonder about them out loud.

"Rode into town yesterday 'long about sundown," Watrous remarked, rocking a bit on his worndown bootheels, and shuttling his appraising gaze between Toby Clarkin and Howie Dryden who were idling on the narrow planked walk across the wheel-rutted street. "Wonder what brought them here?"

"That's a damned good question, Gil," Haley, a huge hulk of a man, said, hoisting his sagging gunbelt above his potbelly. "And I wish I knew the answer to it. I know we need new blood in this town because it's just about dyin' on its feet. But not their kind o' blood," and the sheriff nodded in the direction of Clarkin and Dryden.

"We-ll, what d'you make of them?" the deputy, a lean six-footer, asked. "I mean, just by looking at th'm?"

"Let's see now. That long, hungry lookin' maverick looks like an out-an'-out drifter and saddle tramp to me. The clothes he's wearing are too big for him and musta been hooked out've somebody's barn or swiped offa washline. He's got a kinda jittery way about him like he's expecting something to happen and it's got him on edge or plain scared."

Watrous grinned at him and said:

"Go on, Neil. You're doing fine. What about the other one? How've you got him sized up?"

"I can't tell much about him just by lookin' at him 'cept that I don't like his looks any more'n I do his skinny partner's. I'm basing that opinion, we-ll, on general principles of judging a man by the company he keeps, and that skinny one looks like the troublesome kind."

"All right, Neil. So what d'we do?" Watrous wanted to know.

"We don't do anything," the sheriff replied. "We don't have to. We'll kinda stand by and wait for them to do something. We'll keep an eye on th'm, and the first wrong move they make, that'll be their last. Leastways in Starbuck. We'll grab them and chase them the hell outta town, jump them so fast, they won't know what hit them."

"Right," the deputy said with a nod and hitched up his belt and quite mechanically patted the holstered gun that rode on his right thigh.

Had the lawmen been within earshot of the two objects of their interest, they would not have delayed taking action against them beyond the time it would have taken them to cross the street that separated them. As they stood together backed against the dirt smudged and rain streaked window of a vacant store, Clarkin said to Dryden:

"I've seen more life in a graveyard than I have here. So I dunno whether we're wasting our time here or not. No way of knowing if there's any real dough here. Wish to hell they had a bank. That would have made things interesting. But according to that bartender down the street, the nearest bank is nearly fifty miles from here. So it figures that people aimin' to deposit anything, the storekeepers that is, then they must have to send their dough by stage. If that's the way it is here, then the only way we can hope to do ourselves any good is for us to bushwhack the stage once it gets outta town. What d'you think?"

Dryden didn't answer. His rounded shoulders lifted in an empty shrug and Clarkin leveled a curious look at him.

"Don't you ever have any ideas on anything?" he asked.

"Sure," Dryden replied. "But yours seem to be better. So I chuck mine and go along with your ideas."

Clarkin shook his head.

"You're the damnedest feller I've ever met up with," he said. "I never know for sure what you're thinking or how to figure you."

"Don't look now," Dryden told him low-voiced out of a corner of his mouth, "but those two across the street in the sheriff's office . . ."

"Yeah? What about them?" Clarkin asked quickly, stealing a guarded look through the spread fingers of the hand that he raised to his eyes as though he sought to shield them from the daylight.

"They've been watching us and I'll bet they're talking about us too."

"The hell with th'm," Clarkin said. "We aren't doing anything. There's no law that I ever heard tell of against people standing around and talking. So let them look and talk." He rubbed his chin and then his jaw with the back of his hand. "I'm gonna go get me a shave and a haircut. Don't wanna scare off any likely lookin' woman who might be looking for somebody to get cozy with. Wanna come along, or you wanna stay put here and wait till I get duded up?"

"I'll wait."

Clarkin nodded and turning away from him started up the street, stopped and looked back at him over his shoulder, grinned at him and said:

"Now don't go pullin' anything by yourself. But if you do, remember we're partners and that I get half of what the take comes to."

"I'll remember," Dryden answered gravely.

Squaring around with what was doubtless an unconscious heave of his body, Clarkin marched up the street. Dryden, half-turning, ranged his eyes after him, saw him near the far corner, slant across the walk and enter the barber shop. As Dryden eased around again, a man who rode tall in the saddle came jogging along, pulled up in front of the sheriff's office and dismounted, tied up his horse at the hitchrail and sauntered inside. There was something vaguely familiar about the man. Because he readily admitted that his memory wasn't very good, the unexpected sight of someone who looked familiar but whom he couldn't place, bothered Dryden. A frown mirrored his feelings. But boldly leveling a full look at the sheriff's office, he saw the two lawmen and the newcomer talking together. But when the three turned and looked squarely at him through the window, Dryden flushed, hastily averted his gaze and raising his eyes, looked up at the sky. He was startled when he suddenly became aware of someone coming across the street toward him. Still flush-faced, he jerked his head around. The tall newcomer stepped up on the walk.

"Hello," he said with a friendly smile.

"H-h'llo," Dryden responded.

129

"You don't remember me, do you?"

"N-o, can't say I do," Dryden replied a little falteringly, and began to feel a bit sick to his stomach.

"Well, let's see if I can refresh your memory," the tall man said. "The name of the town was Macum and some of the people there, Andy Horvath, Lars Thielesen and Jesse Twombly who happens to be my uncle, and Kelsey Peters among a lot of others, and a young squirt named Clete Ainslee who ..."

"Oh, sure!" Dryden said excitedly, interrupting him, and because he was relieved, he laughed, a little nervously but happily. " 'Course I remember you. You're Ed Twombly and you're a marshal. Right?"

"Right," Twombly said and they shook hands. "When I get back to Macum and I tell the folks there that I ran into you, they'll hang on every word I say. They liked you, Dryden, liked you a lot, and they won't forget you in a hurry. By the way," and he looked back at the two lawmen who were still watching them through the sheriff's window, "they've been wondering about you, a stranger, and what might have brought you here. When I got a good look at you, I recognized you right off, and when I told them about you and Macum, they were mighty relieved."

"Oh," Dryden said.

"Small towns, you know, are always suspicious of strangers and Starbuck's no exception," the marshal continued. "Want to ask you something, Dryden, if you don't mind. Your good friends in Macum couldn't understand why you slipped away without letting any of them know why you were leaving."

"Guess you know they wanted to make me sheriff, huh?"

Twombly nodded and commented:

"That was their way of showing you how much they thought of you."

"And I'm sure grateful to them all, every last one of them too. Never met a nicer bunch of people anywhere, and I'd like you to tell them that, Marshal, the next time you see them. But that was no job for me and I wasn't the man for the job. It takes a special kind of man, I think, to be a lawman, and because I know better'n anybody else what I'm capable of doing and what I'm not up to doing or even taking on, I slipped out've Andy Horvath's place while they were having themselves a time celebrating, got my horse and lit out. But you tell them for me, please, Marshal, the next time you hit Macum that I didn't mean to, we-ll, offend any of them. I wouldn't do that to anybody, least of all them. All right?"

"Sure thing, Dryden. I understand and when I tell them I know they'll understand too." They stood facing each other in silence for a brief moment. Then Twombly asked: "How are things going for you?"

"O-h, so so."

"Uh-huh. Use a couple o' bucks, Dryden? I can spare it and you can take your time paying it back. How about it?"

Dryden smiled and shook his head.

"Mighty decent of you to offer, Marshal, and I appreciate it. But I can make out all right. But thanks anyway."

"Whatever you say. O-h, you aiming to stay put in Starbuck? If you are, I've got some friends here and I'll be glad to ask around if you're looking for a job. Just say the word."

"Thanks, but I'm not plannin' to stay around. Fact is, I'm just passing through on my way to California."

"Oh, I see! California, huh?"

"Got nothing to keep me here, so . . ."

"Well, good luck to you," the tall man said and thrust out his hand to Dryden who gripped it as before, "but if California doesn't turn out to be all you expect it to be, you've got some mighty good friends who'd be real glad to have you come back to them. You might keep that in mind just in case, y'know?"

Dryden nodded and said: "I know."

"So long."

"So long, Marshal."

Twombly stepped back, flashed Dryden a parting smile and a half-salute, turned on his heel and went striding back across the street to the sheriff's office. Following him with his eyes, the frightening thought came suddenly but belatedly to Dryden that he had missed his chance, probably the best chance he might ever get, of getting away from Toby Clarkin. Now it was too late, for Clarkin would be

131

returning to his side at any moment. Clarkin, who had long committed himself to a life of crime, by partnering himself with Dryden was condemning the latter to the same fate that would eventually befall him. For a fleeting moment, just as Twombly neared the door to Neil Haley's office, Dryden was tempted to dash after him, stop him and blurt out what he knew about Clarkin. The law would take it from there and he would be saved from trouble and very likely from a rope. He stopped instantly in his tracks after he had taken a single step toward the low wooden curb for someone came sidling up to him, nudged him and asked:

"Who was that?"

Dryden swallowed hard. Slowly, almost reluctantly, he turned his head. Toby Clarkin, clean shaven and shiny faced and smelling of some kind of scented water, was standing at his elbow.

"Get your self all duded up so quick?" Dryden asked.

"Never mind about that," Clarkin retorted. "Who was that big feller and what'd he want?"

"O-h, him?" Dryden asked with a nod in the general direction of the sheriff's office.

"Yeah," Clarkin said curtly. "Him."

"His name is Twombly. Ed Twombly."

"That's nice. What'd he want?" Clarkin pressed Dryden.

"He didn't want anything 'cept to say 'hello'."

"Then that musta been the longest 'hello' on record."

"O-h, we talked some about people we both know."

"You get around to asking him anything that we wanna know?"

Dryden shook his head and added an unnecessary 'Nope'.

"You could've, couldn't you, then why didn't you?" Clarkin demanded, his angry tone reflecting his annoyance with Dryden. "I dunno what the hell is the matter with you, passing up a chance like that. I'm beginning to think I've saddled myself with a . . . a deadhead."

"Could be," Dryden said calmly, meeting Clarkin's angry eyes. "But you're forgetting something."

"I am, huh?"

"Yeah. I didn't ask for this. I woulda made it all right to California by myself. But you decided we'd make it together, and there wasn't anything I could do about it."

Clarkin's eyes burned into Dryden's. But he controlled himself and asked evenly:

"You mind telling me why you didn't ask that Twombly or whatever his name is something that woulda been helpful to us?"

"I don't mind at all. It just happens that Ed Twombly's a U. S. marshal and nobody goes asking a marshal the kind of questions you wanna have answers to. I know I wouldn't. But you can if you wanna. All you have to do is go across the street."

Clarkin studied Dryden's angular face for a moment. Then he said:

"I don't know what to do about you, Dryden. I'll have to think about it."

"I've done my thinking about us already, so I can tell you right here and now what I'm gonna do about you."

Head tilted, Clarkin eyed him obliquely.

"Yeah?"

"We're parting company, you an' me, and we're doing it as of now. You gimme back my gun and I'll give you yours. Then you can go your way and I'll go mine. And you don't have to worry none that the moment you go off that I'll go hotfootin' it across the street and tell the marshal so he can go after you. Like I told you in the beginning, I don't run off at the mouth and I don't talk outta turn."

"Now hold it a minute, Dryden. I think we oughta talk this thing out. Then if we can't fix things up between us, all right. We'll split up like you say. But I don't like talkin' out in the street. I like a little privacy, y'know? So suppose we go get our horses and ride out and pick us a spot where we can each speak our piece and with nobody around to horn in? All right?"

"Nope, no deal," Dryden said quietly. "I'm stayin' right here, right where I've got the law to protect me. Here you won't dare try to gun me down because you know what'll happen to you a minute after. I may be as dumb as all get-out. But I've got enough sense to know what'd happen to me if I was fool enough to ride out with you. How about my gun?"

"I'm keeping it," Clarkin said flatly.

"Just like that, huh?"

"Yeah, just like that. 'Less you think you're man enough to try 'n take it away from me."

"I don't have to because I know I'll get it back same's I've always got it back before. Everybody who's ever taken it offa me has died hard and that includes a woman and she got what was coming to her same's the others did. And you will too. I know you won't believe this, Clarkin, but I'll tell it to you anyway because I'll feel better knowing that I warned you. There's a curse on that gun. But if you think you can beat it, it's all right with me. Only you won't beat it anymore'n the others did."

Clarkin grinned evilly, his teeth even more yellowish than ordinarily, probably because of the contrasting effect of his smooth-shaven and shiny face.

"You'll have to do a helluva lot better'n that, Dryden," he answered. "I don't scare easy. What's more, I don't believe in curses or ghosts." He settled his hat securely on his head and hitched up his belt, patted the holstered gun that was tied down around his right thigh, and said with a significance that was not lost on Dryden: "Maybe I'll see you again somewhere, huh?"

"Maybe," Dryden said, although he hoped fervently that it would never come to pass.

Clarkin gave him a sneery look and strode off down the street to the stable where they had left their horses. Holding his gaze on him, Dryden saw him cut across the walk, turn into and disappear down the length of the alley that led to the stable. Minutes passed. Then Dryden saw him ride out to the street, halt and twist around and look back at him. Then squaring around and settling himself in the saddle he loped away. He reached the far corner shortly, pulled up to permit a bonneted woman with a marketing basket swinging from her wrist to cross the street in front of him. Then he rode on, took the westward road and disappeared from sight.

"Hope to hell I'm wrong," Dryden murmured. "But I've got the feeling that I haven't seen the last of him."

SEVENTEEN

The once-a-week westbound stage, with Trumbull the county seat some forty miles away its first stop after a night's layover and a change of horses at Mitch Heneke's station, had but one passenger abroad, and he was a non-paying passenger at that. He was Sheriff Neil Haley who was making his weekly trip to the bank in Trumbull to deposit various amounts of money for Starbuck's store-keepers. Each man's deposit was contained in a thong-tied canvas bag that bore his name, courtesy of the bank. An even dozen bags half-filled a gunny sack that Haley had brought aboard with him and which he had placed between his feet as he lay back, his relaxed bulk filling and almost overflowing the entire front-facing seat. The driver of the stage was a leathery-faced, gravel-voiced in-dividual named Tom McNeely.

"Nice day, huh, Sheriff?" the latter yelled.

"Yeah," Haley answered, but because he was a cautious man he was reluctant to commit himself to an unqualified opinion on anything till he was thoroughly confident and certain too that nothing could possibly go wrong. Experi-ence had taught him that it wasn't wise to accept some-one else's assurances particularly when that someone else wasn't qualified to offer them too freely. So he added rather wryly: "Nice so far."

"Heck," McNeely yelled. He had to raise his voice even louder this time in an effort to be heard above the echoing metallic clatter of his four horses' ironshod hoofs as they pranced and strained and hauled the squeaky bodied stage up a stony incline and then into a narrow, wagon-wide pass. Here the going was even rougher for the pass was rock-and-boulder lined and studded with half-buried and upended rocks. It was impossible for any kind of vehicle wending its way through the pass to avoid jouncing its passengers. "Heck," McNeely repeated. "You've been makin' this same gol-darned run every week for the past three years and nothin's happened to you yet."

"I know," the sheriff yelled back at him. "But there's always a first time for everything, y'know, and this could be it."

McNeely didn't answer, a sign that he was otherwise occupied.

"Take it easy, willyuh, Tom?" Haley yelled. "My breakfast is up in my throat."

To lessen the jouncing, McNeely slowed the horses to a walk. The pass was a comparatively short one, probably no more than thirty or forty feet long. When the stage emerged from it, there was a downgrade to be negotiated that was just as stony as the upgrade. But inside the pass some of the rock piles were so high that the sheriff who was hunched forward and resting his left elbow on the paneless door sill couldn't see above them.

"Doggone it, Tom, what are you tryin' t'do?" he yelled in protest when a half-buried rock refused to yield to the stagecoach's left front wheel which caromed off the rock, came at it a second time and rolled over it, and came thudding down on the ground with such force that the stage lurched crazily. Despite his weight and his awing bulk, Haley was propelled upward from his seat, crushing his hat into a flat mass when his head collided with the vehicle's low ceiling. Dropping back into his seat and reshaping his hat, he yelled: "Why'n thunder don't you get that penny-pinchin' outfit you work for to spend a few bucks and turn this pass into something fit for people to ride through, huh? Wouldn't cost such a helluva lot to hire a couple o' men and horses and some chains and do a job in here. And once they got finished levelin' off the ground they could haul out some o' these rocks and boulders from along the sides and give you some room so you wouldn't go scrapin' your wheels on them."

Before the gravel-voiced driver could answer him, another and a more authoritative voice called out:

"All right, driver! Hold it right there!"

In former years holdups in the pass were frequent. Sometimes the holdup man or men obtained a great deal. Sometimes though and about as often, little was obtained.

136

Sometimes when the holdup man, not overly experienced, rose up from behind some rocks and stepped out unwarily, a blast of pointblank gunfire from some itchy-fingered passenger greeted him and flung him back bullet-riddled and quite dead. But with the passing of time, there was less and less defiance of the law and fewer and fewer holdups and finally there were none. McNeely would have been hard put to recall the last time that the stage had been held up. He had survived them when they had happened with annoying regularity because he had had the good sense to obey the moment he was ordered to pull up, and because he had steadfastly refused to reach for the company issued shotgun that was propped up at his side against his right leg. The company, he maintained, didn't pay him enough to warrant his risking his life. Accordingly he pulled back hard on the lines, bringing the surprised horses and the stage to an abrupt and jouncing stop. He squared back in his seat with his empty hands held high so that the holdup man would see at once that he had nothing to fear from him.

Haley was unprepared for the sudden halt. He was flung forward into the opposite seat and bumped his head hard on the woodwork that framed it. Somewhat dazed when he forced himself back, he poked his head out of the wrong-side window. Before he realized that he had made a mistake, that the voice had come from the other side, and before he was able to turn himself in that direction, a gun was poked in at him and the evil, smirking face of the man holding it on him appeared in the window on the right side. The sheriff recognized the man at once as Howie Dryden's companion. He snorted a little when he recalled the marshal's repeated assurance that Dryden was 'all right'. Clarkin reached in with his left hand, tore Haley's hand away from his gunbutt and yanked the lawman's gun out of the holster and shoved it down inside his pants' belt. Then he reached in again with his left hand.

"Come on," he commanded. "I know you're on your way to the bank, Sheriff. Hand over the dough and make it quick. I wanna get outta here."

"I . . . I don't know what you're talking about," Haley said, a little falteringly though, and flushed.

"You don't, huh?" Clarkin retorted. "That bag between your big flat feet," he said and he pointed to it. "I suppose that's full o' feed for the horses and you're ridin' herd on it for them. Y'better hand it over, Sheriff. I've got me a nervous trigger finger, and sometimes, even before I'm ready for it, it jerks and my gun goes 'bang!' And the one I'm pointing it at gets himself a nice big hole right smack in his belly. And you've got plenty o' belly. So my gun won't miss."

Reluctantly the sheriff reached down, curled a clammy hand around the tied neck of the gunny sack, lifted the sack as he eased himself back in his seat, and handed it to Clarkin. The latter grunted, stepped back with it, and raising his eyes to Tom McNeely said curtly:

"All right, Mac. Drop the shotgun over the side."

McNeely obeyed. The shotgun dropped, stock first, and toppled over on the ground just beyond Clarkin's feet.

"Get going," McNeely was told.

As the relieved driver reached for the reins, the drumming beat of horses' hoofs came from the direction of the upgrade.

"Wait," Clarkin ordered McNeely and the latter sat motionless.

With the gunny sack slung over his left shoulder and his gun raised for a quick shot, Clarkin fixed his gaze on the top of the upgrade. Two horsemen, Marshal Ed Twombly and Howie Dryden, topped the incline and came jogging into the pass. Cursing, Toby Clarkin flung a shot at them, whirled around and darted behind a boulder and hastily crouched down in anticipation of a return shot. But there was none. Apparently surprised and wondering if it meant that they had dismounted and were scrambling toward him over the rocks in hopes of surrounding him and flushing him out, he scowled darkly. In a more or less frenzied attempt to thwart them and avoid being trapped, he crept away on hands and knees to a point about midway between the halted stagecoach and the entrance to the pass. Wheezing and heaving, he took refuge behind a white-faced boulder, huddled there for a moment till he got his breath, then he raised up slowly and cautiously peered out. His eyes widened and his mouth opened a bit too. His wildly pegged and unaimed shot had found the target. The marshal, obviously solidly hit by the bullet, had slipped off or fallen off his horse and was on the ground on his knees, headbowed and hunched over and rocking gently from side to side. Dryden, apparently stunned by what had happened, was still sitting his horse and staring at the wounded lawman. He seemed to be incapable of movement judging by the fact that he made no attempt to climb down and help him.

Clarkin laughed and stepped out recklessly, indicating that he was satisfied that he had nothing more to fear from Twombly, and that he did not consider Dryden a threat to him.

"Now you . . . you bastid!" he raged at Dryden and leveled his gun at him. "Now you're gonna get it! You hadda go and put the law on to me, didn't you? I'm gonna pay you back good for that!"

Dryden's head jerked as he took his eyes from Twombly and lifted them to Clarkin. There was fright in them, the look of a thoroughly terrified and admittedly helpless man who could do nothing to defend himself save plead for his life. He put out his hand but the words that he sought to utter stuck in his throat and choked him. His eyes bulged as he struggled so frantically to down the lump in his throat before it strangled him. They seemed to be clinging to the yawning and ever widening fire-blackened muzzle of the gun as though he were held in terrified fascination by it. He did not appear to be aware of Clarkin's futile efforts to pull the trigger. Fortunately there were no witnesses to what followed, so he had no reason to offer an explanation to anyone. As for himself, he preferred to let it go unexplained for the very thought of it was enough to make him shudder.

He knew he couldn't have been in his right mind to have drawn on a man who was holding a leveled gun on him, and a man who was without question a far better shot than he was. But that was what he did. He could not remember drawing the gun that Clarkin had forced him to accept in exchange for Shattuck's gun. But he agreed that he must have for all of a sudden it was in his hand and he was shooting. Three shots that were fired so closely together that they blended into one thunderous roar burst upon the hapless Toby Clarkin. He staggered and stumbled about blindly as the successive slugs tore into him, flung about like a weed caught in a wind storm. The gunny sack fell at his feet. Then he sagged as his legs gave way under him and he fell brokenly on top of the sack. What Dryden kept to himself and never even hinted at it to anyone was that when he swung down from his horse and ran to Clarkin and took the Shattuck gun out of his numbing hand and looked hard at the gun he saw that it had jammed.

As he dropped Clarkin's half-emptied gun at the latter's feet and holstered the reclaimed Shattuck gun, Sheriff Neil Haley and Tom McNeely, the former with the driver's shotgun in his hands and half-raised for a quick shot, came running from the direction of the stage and skidded to a stop at Dryden's side.

"Got him, huh?" the hulking lawman asked with a glance at the felled Clarkin. "What'd he do with the sack?"

Dryden didn't answer. He simply dragged Clarkin over on his side. Haley, spotting the sack, snatched it up and clutching it to him, pushed the shotgun into McNeely's hands and scurried off to where Ed Twombly lay face downward in the stony dirt. As Dryden and McNeely, following him, gathered around him, Haley dropped the sack on the ground between his feet, bent over the marshal and gently eased him over on his back.

It was some seven or eight weeks later. It was a weekday, the time about six-thirty in the morning. Hence it was still much too early for any of the townspeople or even the storekeepers to be up and about. But there were two men, the town's acknowledged earliest risers, who were up as everyone else expected they would be. However neither of them was an ordinary townsman nor a storekeeper in the usual sense. One was aproned Pat Fry, Deedee Farnum's bartender, who was sweeping off the walk in front of the latter's saloon. The other was the sheriff, stocky and greying Win Tuttle, who was idling in the open doorway of his office, his usual frown clouding his lined face and his thumbs hooked in his belt. Fry stayed his broom and looked around when a horseman with a rifle butt jutting out of his saddleboot and a blanket roll strapped or behind him came jogging up the hushed street. When the

140

man whom Fry did not recognize came abreast of him and rode past him, the bartender followed him with wondering eyes. His brows arched a bit when he saw the man pull up in front of the sheriff's office and dismount. Tuttle, shifting his weight from one leg to the other, despite his pretended disinterest in the man, watched him open his saddlebag and take something out of it. When he turned around Tuttle saw that the object, whatever it was, was wrapped in canvas. As the man came across the walk, the sheriff straightened up.

"Yeah?" he asked. "Something I can do for you, Mister?"

The stranger flipped back his coat and Tuttle glimpsed a star pinned to his shirtfront.

"Oh!" he said. "Marshal, huh? Come in."

The man followed him inside. Tuttle quickly spun a chair away from the wall and set it down in front of his desk, then he moved around the desk to his own chair.

"This your territory now?" he asked, drawing the chair back a bit.

"No. Mine's further west. O-h, my name's Twombly. Ed Twombly. Yours is Tuttle, isn't it?"

"That's right. Sit down, Marshal."

"Thanks," Twombly acknowledged and eased himself down into the chair that Tuttle indicated. He thumbed his hat up from his forehead, leaned forward and placed the canvas-wrapped object on the desk in front of the sheriff, then pushed it even closer to him. "That's for you. That's what brought me here."

"Oh? What is it?"

"Why don't you unwrap it and see for yourself?"

Tuttle grunted, flipped back the canvas wrapping, and stared at the gun that lay before him.

"That's Len Shattuck's gun," he said quickly, and raised his eyes to meet the marshal's. "How'd you come to get it, Marshal? You take it away from that mangy Dryden polecat?"

"Mangy polecat?" Twombly repeated. "That doesn't fit the Howie Dryden I know."

"Long, skinny, hungry-lookin' maverick," Tuttle said. "That what your Dryden looks like?"

The marshal smiled, and his white, even teeth shone in his face.

"That's close enough, I guess. So I think we're talking about the same man even though I don't particularly like the way you described him. Anyway, according to Dryden, you feel that when a gun slinger dies or gets himself killed, his gun should be buried with him. That right?"

"A gun slinger's gun is part of him and the way I look at it both of th'm should be buried at the same time. I don't like the idea of a dead gunny's gun on the loose. Somebody with big ideas might get hold of it and think it's the gun that makes a man a top gun. That what happened to Dryden? He try to make out like he was another Len Shattuck because he had his gun?"

"No," Twombly said with a shake of his head. There was something in his tone that made Tuttle wish he had been more careful in his choice of words, and in his unconcealed and scornful opinion of Dryden. He resolved to make amends at the first opportunity that presented itself. "Dryden never pulled the gun on anyone. Nor did he ever let the gun give him false ideas." Tuttle winced. "However, those who took the gun away from him and tried to use it on him or on others, died violently. There were six who did that, and one of them was a woman."

"H'm," the sheriff said.

"After the last affair, Dryden became convinced that there was a curse on the gun," the marshal continued. "When he asked if I would see to it that it was returned to you, I agreed. I'd have been here sooner. But I had a rather bad bullet wound in my shoulder that took its time healing." Twombly paused. When there was no response from Tuttle, he went on with: "Apparently you don't think very highly of Dryden, Sheriff. So I'd like to tell you what I know about him, how he saved a town from a young gun thrower who tried to take it over, and how he had the nerve to draw on a fugitive who had him covered, o-h, yes, with Shattuck's gun, and killed him. You may think differently about Dryden when I've finished."

Seizing upon this as a good opportunity to begin making amends, Tuttle said with a smile, something that was most unusual for him:

"I'm listening, Marshal. I'm big enough to admit I've made a mistake when I find I've sized up a man all wrong."

He listened attentively to Twombly's recital of Dryden's

exploits, and when the marshal finished and sat back in his chair, Tuttle sat back too, shaking his head.

"Never thought he had that in him," he said. "But y'know something, Marshal? I'm damned glad to know it. Must be when you know a man too long, you kinda lose sight of his good qualities and all you ever think of are his . . . his, we-ll, what you think are his shortcomings. Right?"

"You may have something there," Twombly conceded.

"Where's Howie now?" the sheriff asked, and the marshal smiled a little to himself.

"Last I saw of him he was headed for California. He should be there by now."

"Hope he makes out all right there."

"He will," Twombly assured him. "I gave him the names of a couple of good friends of mine who live in California and told him where he could find them. They're good, solid citizens. Influential ones too. They'll take him in tow. So I know he'll make out just fine."

When he stood up and settled his hat on his head, Tuttle rose too and came out from behind his desk.

"You figure you'll hear from him?" he asked.

"Y-es, I think so. Why, Sheriff? Why do you ask?"

"I'll tell you why, Marshal. This town is dyin' on its feet and being that nobody seems to care one way or another, I don't see 'ny point in me stayin' around here any longer. I'm not that old that I can't move on somewhere's else and find me something to do to earn my keep."

"Uh-huh."

"Couple of us, the bartender across the street, the stable man and two or three others, none of us with any kind of family ties to hold us back, we've been talking about it and we've decided to cut outta here come next Spring and go somewhere's else. Some place that's new and big and where we'd have a chance to do something for ourselves. Y'know?"

"Like California?"

"That's right," Tuttle said instantly. "Fact is, we're pretty well decided on California."

"So?" Twombly asked with a knowing smile.

"We-ll, when you hear from Dryden, that is from Howie, I'd sure appreciate it if you'd let him know that some of his friends'll be heading out his way in a couple o' months

143

and because they'll be right glad to see him again, they aim to look him up when they hit California."

The marshall made no comment.

"Being that he'll be pretty well set himself, could be he might be willing to give us a lead on to something. Y'know?"

"Uh-huh."

"Had your breakfast yet, Marshal? Don't suppose so, huh? Then how about having it with me? Give us a chance to get better acquainted and at the same time you might give me the names of the people Howie'll be stayin' with and where we can find them. O-h, if you wanna wash up, I've got a clean towel you can use."

When Tuttle turned and led the way to the back room, his living quarters, Ed Twombly, with a tiny smile still wrinkling the corners of his mouth, trooped after him.